OTHER BOOKS BY MARJORIE MADDOX

True, False, None of the Above

Wives' Tales

Inside Out: Poems on Writing Poems

A Man Named Branch: The True Story of Baseball's Great Experiment

Local News from Someplace Else

Rules of the Game: Baseball Poems

A Crossing of Zebras: Animal Packs in Poetry

Weeknights at the Cathedral

Common Wealth: Contemporary Poets on Pennsylvania (co-editor)

Transplant, Transport, Transubstantiation

Perpendicular As I

When the Wood Clacks Out Your Name: Baseball Poems

Body Parts

Ecclesia

How to Fit God into a Poem

Nightrider to Edinburgh

For more information,
please see www.marjoriemaddox.com

WHAT SHE WAS SAYING

Stories

Marjorie Maddox

Fomite

Burlington, VT

Copyright © 2014 by the University of Nebraska Press. "And Then" by Marjorie Maddox is reprinted by permission from *Frontiers: A Journal of Women Studies* 37, no. 2.

Copyright © 2005 by the *Christian Century.* "Lot's Daughters" (in an earlier version) by Marjorie Maddox is reprinted by permission from the 6 September 2005 issue of the *Christian Century.*

Copyright © 2008 by Sport Literature Association. "For Real" by Marjorie Maddox is reprinted by permission from the 22 March 2007 issue of *Aethlon: The Journal of Sport Literature.*

Copyright © 2016 by the University of Nebraska Press. "Soldier Girl" by Marjorie Maddox is reprinted by permission from *Frontiers: A Journal of Women Studies* 37, no. 2.

ISBN-13: 978-1-942515-68-5
Library of Congress Control Number: 2016957271

Author Photo: Dawn Snyder
Cover Image: Global Adventures/iStock
Cover Design: Gary R. Hafer

Fomite
58 Peru Street
Burlington, VT 05401
www.fomitepress.com

To my sister, Ann,
and my daughter, Anna Lee—
may your voices be ever strong.

Acknowledgments

The author gratefully acknowledges the following publications, where stories first appeared.

"And Then," *Frontiers: A Journal of Women Studies*

"Articulate," *Cider Press Review* and *Reconfigurations*

"Best Face Forward," *Ellipsis* (Wayward Couch Press)

"Birthday Cake," *The Doctor T. J. Eckleburg Review*

"Crowned," *Dirt: An Anthology* (The New Yinzer Press) and *The Lascaux Prize 2015 Anthology* (finalist for The Lascaux Prize in Short Fiction 2015)

"Communion of the Saints," *Relief Magazine*

"Dog Days," *To Unsnare Time's Warp* (A Main Street Rag Anthology)

"*A Doll's House* Redux," *Midway Journal*

"Eiffel Tower," *Modern Language Studies* and finalist for the Gertrude Stein Award in Fiction 2015, sponsored by *The Doctor T. J. Eckleburg Review*

"Exhibition," *The Art Times*

"For Real" (winner of the 2007 Sport Literature Association Fiction Award), *Aethlon: The Journal of Sport Literature*

"Front Door/Back Door," *Pinyon Review's* 2016 Commemorative Issue

"Learning to Yell," *The Medulla Review*

"Lost," *Prime Number*

"Lot's Daughters," *Christian Century*

"Nonsmoking Section" (nominated for a 2011 Pushcart Prize), *The Minnesota Review*

"Pennsylvania Round in Four Parts," *Watershed* and *Not Somewhere Else But Here: A Contemporary Anthology of Women and Place* (Sundress Publications)

"Permanent," *The Doctor T. J. Eckleburg Review*

"Rachel Isum Robinson: Snatches and Excerpts," *African American Review*

"Rough Drafts," *The Other Journal*

"Seagulls" (nominated for a 1995 Pushcart Prize), *The American Literary Review*

"Soldier Girl," *Frontiers: A Journal of Women Studies*

"Some Women Fall in Love With Criminals," *Arabesques Review*

"Squirrelly in PA," *Watershed* and *Western Pennsylvania Reflections: Stories from the Alleghenies to Lake Erie* (The History Press)

"UPS Guy," *Dime Show Review*

"Watching *42* at the Dollar Matinee with My Mother," *The Cresset*

"Water," *SLAB Literary Magazine*

"A Wave Rushed Over" (2007 fiction prize), *US Catholic*

"Weeds," *Cream City Review* and *Great Stream Review*

"What She Hears," *The Battered Suitcase* (Vagabond Press)

"What She Was Saying," *The Sonora Review*

"The Wives" (in a previous version), *Wives' Tales* (Seven Kitchens Press), as well as the excerpts "Peter, Peter," "Piper," "Rabbit," *Seattle Review* (in an earlier version winner of the 1993 *Seattle Review's* Bentley Prize for Poetry)

"Woman's First Skydive Turns Out to Be Her Last," *SLAB Literary Magazine*

I would like to give additional thanks to my colleague, Dana Washington, and my sister, Ann Silvey, for their steadfast moral support; my daughter, Anna Lee, and my son, Will, for their honest feedback; my husband, Gary R. Hafer, not only for his graphic design and editorial expertise, but also for his willingness to hear *What* [this woman] *Was Saying*; and for Marc Estrin and Donna Bister for believing enough to set these tales in book form before the world.

Articulate,

I'm not, all fine-toed thought
tip-tripping on this gangplank of tongue,
clumsy and cumbersome in the outside air
of others' ears and expectations;
all incubation of consonants off-limits,
sounds' syllables looking silly
without a line to dry on.
What a mess of metaphors the mouth makes!
It's the pen that injects
tap dance, the click-clack of keys
that decodes the meaning.
Outside the letters, I'm incognito.
A suburbanite. Two toddlers.
A mouthful of stumbling practicality.
You won't see me
till I write.

CONTENTS

CROWNED

PUMPKIN, APPLE, SORGHUM, BLUEBERRY—I do all the festivals. Judge giant pies the size of wading pools. Win goldfish religiously. Sip milkshakes as thick as all my wishes. At each one, I am the queen, a half-wave to the left, a half-wave to the right, riding on a shiny John Deere or a customized Cadillac while my court follows on Harleys or streamered pick-ups. What does the rest of my life matter when I have a basket of berries, when 4-H kids stand on their tiptoes and point at my crown?

You don't have to be television-pretty. I am the preacher's kid and have twenty-three freckles on my face, one for each of my talents, my daddy says. I think it's for the times we'll move in and out of duplexes, refurbished garages, or a parsonage in need of electricity and paint. We arrive well before the voting when any new girl is cute enough and a minister's someone important, his wife voted to every committee.

But there's only Daddy and I and the empty slots for Dog-Sled or Quilting Festival Queen. My hair is long, shiny, uncut. Daddy says that's the crown of any girl, that and a Christian way of being, honest-like and full of thank-you's. I catch on quick, remember how Mama was before the baby that took them both. It wasn't Jesus that did it. He let his mama live. Saved her one of the biggest crowns in heaven. My mama has one too, I'm sure—sparkled as sweetness. But I don't think the baby's there, seeing what she did by trying to be born too quickly. She should have waited her turn.

Daddy and I know about taking turns. When he sees someone at the convenience store, scowling as he sorts through the Shop Mart guides, Daddy says to me, "This one is yours. Turn on that pretty smile and tell him about Jesus." When he sees a new bank teller or the secretary at the town insurance company, he says, "This one is mine" and smiles big as eternity. Then he gives her directions to church and our number. We know what's to be done. If you're not nice, there's nobody to fill the pews. It's the job, and we work quickly. "There's only so many days before Jesus comes back," Daddy says each time he sees a new clerk at the Coastal Mart.

Time keeps moving, and people move with it. Knowing that makes it easy. People will wave goodbye in a few months anyway no matter what. The first Sunday they return all our smiles. The next Sunday, too. The months after that, their smiles loosen a bit each time they shut the church door and walk back to their own lives. I know because of what my daddy knows: how their pity reminds them of their own pain, and their pain embarrasses them.

At first, they bring Daddy's favorite casseroles, though I cook just fine. Next, they bring stories of their mothers and their own losses, hidden inside bites of upside-down cake. Finally, they forget about us and our lives. They want us to forget about theirs. They look away, trying to erase their calls at midnight, their shaky voices, and the lives they don't put on parade. I watch them during my solos of "When the Saints Come Marching In." By the last notes, they don't remember my festival crown. They see instead my father's eyes and the slant of his nose; they remember the words he's heard.

I hear some of them, too, though I'm not supposed to. What can I do when Sally Moore's mother arrives red-eyed on the doorstep, a bruise tattooing her arm? She needs my daddy to listen, so I go for the ice. Her words heave between a chorus of sobs. "It's only sometimes," she says, her voice not

2

believing itself. When my daddy's strong arm goes around her, she calms a bit, but keeps talking. Her life comes out of her lips: how her own daddy was, where she'd lived. She was even a festival queen like me, but only once. My own breath comes fast as I wait for her to finish the hard part. She says what has been stuck inside too long: the way she got the baby before she should have. How she married quick, without even a proper dress or a daddy who would give her away. It's then my daddy whispers Bible verses in her ear, the way he did to me when I was a little girl. When I look down, the ice is dripping tiny puddles at my feet. I let it dry up by itself and head to the bedroom.

The next week the plant closes, and Bob Harker sobs on Daddy's shoulder right in the middle of the hardware store. I have the basket with all the stuff we're buying: a new roll of screen for the backdoor to keep the flies out, more oil for the squeaky door hinge that wakes me up each time Daddy has to go out at night. Standing in line with some rope, Mr. Harker sees Daddy and his eyes well up. Then the crying starts. Loud. Even Julie, the cash register girl, knows to look away. Daddy takes him by the shoulder and walks him over by the electric saws where no one else is. They're gone long enough for me to go up and down most of the aisles three times. Then I just sit up front by the Child Safety display and work on my memory verses. When I get done with that, I practice my festival speech, quiet-like so no one can hear. I even practice the hand gestures, imagining the audience. At the end, I look up, thinking how light the new crown will feel.

It's almost closing time when Daddy and Mr. Harker come out. The rope's gone. Instead, Daddy's got us a new welcome mat and holds it up to show me. He shakes Mr. Harker's hand, as if nothing's happened, says he'll see him at church.

We're a team like that, Daddy and I. We're the 1 + 1 = 2 for Noah's ark. We're a right foot and a left foot to march around Jericho. We're the hands to pick the wheat for the holy harvest. So when Freddy Schmidt smashes the family car into the front of Greeley's Garage six hours before Sunday School, we both go. It's just across the street and down a bit, and the ambulance sirens blast through the walls of our tiny house and into the one bedroom. Daddy's up first, tugging on some shorts and a WWJD T-shirt. Quick, like that; then he's out the door. I'm right behind him with some shorts over my nightie. No time for a bra.

When we get there, the ambulance guys are prying Freddy out of the Buick. He's dazed and bleeding across his forehead, Jesus-style. The garage storefront is a mess. Glass everywhere. The car is propped up like those modern sculptures they have at the museums, the front end smashed in like a flattened milk carton. One tire is still spinning. A poster that reads "Change Your Oil. It's Sooner Than You Think" hangs crookedly from what's left of the one wall. There's no alarm, this being a small town, but the neighbors have all come out from across the street and stare at the wreck. They're comparing raising-kid stories, I think. Daddy waves at them, then holds his praying hands up high. The ambulance lights flash across his fingers. It's then I think Freddy looks at me, just for a second, smiling as they carry him off on the stretcher.

We get to the hospital even before his parents, and Daddy puts me on door watch. It's only a few minutes before the Schmidts come rounding the corner in the other car, the one mostly she uses, a rusted-out Toyota. Mr. Schmidt is driving too fast (who wouldn't?), but the parking lot is pretty empty, so there's lots of space to make up for the bad turns and the speed. He parks crooked, taking up two spaces, and they're out and running in. She's got on a nightgown and shorts like I do; he's dressed like Daddy but with a Harley T-shirt. They almost don't see me, but I know enough to run with them, pointing toward a doctor and Daddy. Just like on TV, only better. My daddy's there for Mrs. Schmidt to wrap her arms

4

around. She's crying hysterically and even reaches for my hand twice. It's a good morning, considering. Freddy ends up OK, and Daddy takes me out to Perkins before Sunday School. I get hash browns, pancakes, and scrambled eggs. The waitress recognizes me from my picture in the paper.

* * *

In every town, that's how it starts. In the next weeks, grateful choruses of Amen's will punctuate the sermons. They'll be Sunday supper invitations, strong handshakes, and kisses on the cheek. What follows are the shopping lists jotted on the back of bulletins, the kids-have-a-cold excuses, and the rushed goodbyes. After that, the complaints: sermons too long, budget too high, attendance too low, building too cold.

So before all that, I try to remember the parades. I hold the day in my head like a prayer and deeply inhale the peanut-greasy-fries-caramel-apple smell that circles everyone in town halo-style. I look and see the not-yet familiar faces, unscrubbed for Sunday but breaking with the same other-worldliness that hymns give, a sudden note of joy that takes you from a job you hate and lets you breathe in and out without thinking. The kids are happy and kiss their mothers. The parents hold hands. Most of them recognize me and wave. Like my daddy, I am up front, where everybody looks. I think my crown shimmers like the heavenly ones.

It's the same in every town, wherever we go. The parade rides down whatever the largest street is, past whatever church has hired Daddy, and up toward some rented Ferris wheel where chips of rust float like confetti out over the game barkers. Someone will offer to win me a giant teddy bear or a new Bible, but I'll be listening to the marching band's last song—brash and off-key—the town fire engines shrieking their sirens, prophesying, as I do, what is coming. Because I know.

Daddy says talent is God-given, but I know it's just memorizing the patterns, the important dates, the order and kinds of parades, and what to do when it rains. I can sing and dance OK. I can ride a unicycle without breaking my leg. I can even do three back flips in a row, but that's not what wins me my crown. I know what people want by looking at them. I know who will let out the pain, who will want someone else to feel it. They see a motherless girl and they think, "She knows." They see a man without a wife, and they think, "He knows." It's in their eyes just when they finish smiling hello. It's in what's left of their voices after they shake hands, like an aftertaste that won't go away. That's how it was with Miss Samuels—even before she brought the pies wrapped up with a ribbon.

And the others, the ones who already have kids, they think I am more grateful than their own children. Maybe I am. I have less time and take what I can. I sing "Danny Boy" for Mrs. McCleary, recite the twenty-third Psalm for Joe Johnston, and tap dance "Yankee Doodle Dandy" for old Mr. Abernathy. "What a lovely girl," they say, then listen closely to my daddy's sermons, his voice as earnest as a carnival boy hawking frozen bananas, but kinder.

I want them to listen, but not closely. Not enough to repent. When they repent, they only do so half-heartedly, even when they mean it at the time. They walk down that aisle at the altar call and want to be different. When they walk back, they think they are. When they walk out the big double doors, a little wears off, but not much. When they walk back for Wednesday service, they're sure they've got it down, but then they hear Daddy's soft voice. They remember something they didn't do that they should have or something they shouldn't have done that they did, and they walk down the aisle again. The next week it's a little harder and a little harder still after that.

By the time five Sundays have passed, Mrs. Moore has another bruise, only this time just her eyes say something. Part of what they say is shame. Her husband is an elder. They always are. His eyes say embarrassed. They say, forget what you know.

That's what my eyes used to say every time the congregation decided we knew too much. What the people told us was different: They didn't have enough to pay; or Daddy's sermons weren't good enough; or they got a full-time pastor, one with a wife and five girls, all pretty. These days, my eyes aren't embarrassed. There's always another town, another festival, or another parade with unfamiliar faces. At least that's what I tell myself each night when I'm supposed to be saying my prayers.

This month it's Millville and the Strawberry Festival. The people have different names, but inside they're mostly the same. We arrive on a Thursday in May—after the Coal Festival in Blossburg and before the Corn Festival in wherever we end up next. By the next Tuesday, after Daddy's sweet-voice sermon and my solo on Sunday, I am nominated and out back of the Town Hall being questioned by the judges. It's the first thing in the morning. My freckles are a plus. In the sun, my hair looks a little red, so I'm a natural for the part. The church is a festival sponsor, though most of its girls are too young or too old. Wholesome is what this group wants, a good example for its youth.

After a dozen or so towns, I know the part. I wear a handsewn blouse from the last town's ladies' circle, sky blue the color of innocence with a large strawberry for each collar. The shirt flattens my breasts and falls halfway down my calf-length skirt. It's the right choice. I quote a poem from a Hallmark Mother's Day card. Then, to the tune of "We Gather Together," I trill a song about the town. It's a quick revision to what I performed four towns back. I hold out the last notes long and loud, then smile with all my teeth. The men look at their wives for their reactions. The women nod approvingly.

When the first weekend in June rolls around, Daddy is still the man up front in the pulpit. I am still the new festival queen. We are riding high, getting ready for my crown. Three new families have joined the church. The offering is up. Crops are good. We've had supper invitations each week, twice from Miss Samuels, who, she reminds us again though we don't need telling, makes the best pies in town.

Daddy is preaching on the fruits of the Spirit, and the older ladies are trying to identify who has what gift. Three of the younger girls are my court; they smile like junior bridesmaids and wear their hair like mine, a braid twirled into a loose bun, like a hat slipped to the back of the head. One of the girl's grandmother makes us matching red-gingham dresses with a sash the color of vines.

In the parade, we're up front—where we should be. This time, Daddy, the girls, and I all ride in the same car: a maroon Thunderbird convertible from Walter's backyard mechanic shop. One of the doors is blue and rusting. There are crepe-paper leaves draped across the sides. The girls are scrunched together in the back like triplets, and I ride up front with Daddy, who turns the key as if he's young again and heading out on his honeymoon. My winner's banner is tight, and, because it's hot, the ribbon sticks a bit at my shoulder. The *S* in Strawberry Queen is partly gone and looks like a backwards *c*. I don't mind.

I've clipped the gold-sprayed crown in place with bobby pins, but if I wave too vigorously, it tips a bit, back and forth. I try to keep my head straight, yet there's too much to see. The booths are lined up outside the church and down the street: strawberry ice cream, strawberry shortcake, strawberry cupcakes in ice-cream cones, strawberry pudding, strawberry soda, strawberry crêpes. There's a booth for weaving strawberry placemats and another one for selling strawberry air freshener. A woman on the corner, not a churchgoer, holds up strawberry pinwheels and lets them spin in the wind.

Daddy drives us past slowly. I breathe in the redness, pick out faces in the crowded patch of near-strangers. Then there are the others, the ones who've told us too much. They wave, too.

The high school band blasts "In the Good Old Summertime," hold their heads high, and bounce their knees up to their chests. Just behind us, six- and seven-year-olds, dressed like strawberries, do cartwheels and flips for the clapping bystanders. It's time for me to throw candy, so I reach in one of my baskets and pull out strawberry taffy, each piece attached to a pink curl of paper with a different fruit of the Spirit and a Bible reference penned in neat calligraphy. A crowned missionary, I'm spreading the Word!

Then Daddy turns the wheel and heads us to the town square where a merry-go-round twirls its fantasy promises in the middle of a large circle of park benches. I want doves, but they've flown away. A few sparrows twitter in their place, trying to keep tune with the ponies. At the stand next to the strawberry fritters, past the Tunnel of Love and Monster Scare Shack, Miss Samuels stands outside her red-checkered booth with her pies stacked neatly inside, away from the heat. Her sign is in large, curvy calligraphy, but she's standing so I can't see the price. A single spot of strawberry filling dots her lower lip. When she looks at my daddy, her eyes hold the light, the same way the candles shine in them during Holy Communion. And she is waiting to tell him her life.

I start singing "A Bicycle Built for Two" for my daddy, so he'll look at me instead, but it's too late. He is already waving at Miss Samuels, his left hand high in the air. He forgets he's a preacher. By the time he glances toward me, he's at the corner and takes the turn—even at slow speed—a bit too sharply, just enough so the girls in back say, "Whoa!" The car nudges up against the curb, and I have to steady my crown. When he looks again at me, his face is different. His eyes are a question. For a moment, I forget the sound of his voice. Without his striped tie and white shirt, he's just a regular dad, so I keep my face ahead and smile, looking toward the horizon where I'm sure the next town is hiding, ready to be found, like a strawberry too long in the sun.

What She Was Saying

From the beginning it wasn't right. No beard. Pipe. When Cynthia stepped into his office that first Tuesday, he was standing on a green vinyl chair rehanging a diploma. There were already three nail marks where he'd aimed the hammer. There were other frames below or to the side, documents of one kind or another, a print of the Eiffel tower with a sky a little too blue to be real (obviously retouched), and a photo of a couple in their fifties, about the age of her own parents, smiling one of those We're-Proud-Of-You-Son smiles clear across to the facing blank wall. The eyes of the woman were just a bit crossed. They reminded Cynthia of a caricature of the Mona Lisa, the kind kids add moustaches and glasses on, only this woman had short curly hair and was blond.

But that's not what tipped Cynthia off. The doctor had on no socks. And something else—when he held the picture frame that way (thumb and forefinger like a clip, a flat horizontal print pressed against the glass), the center line stood out too much, the calligraphy too large or dark, but mostly it seemed to be the name: BRENT BEEBE, PH.D all on the same line, the rhyme too forced, the words pushed together like that. In her mind, she substituted Freud or James or Binet—all with enough letters to fill the space—and turned instead to the doctor. "A little to the right," she said, nodding at the diploma. Beebe obeyed.

It took three sessions before he came to her apartment. She was in a peach teddy, rereading the DSM-5, nibbling alternately on peanut butter, crackers, and liver pâté. He stayed thirty-eight minutes and left his glasses. They were round and fragile looking. She put them in the drawer of her bedside table between her diary and a Gideon Bible she'd snatched once from a Holiday Inn in Tulsa. She never mentioned them, and neither did he. But for a few sessions, Beebe squinted more; then, meeting by meeting, his eyebrows relaxed, his forehead unwrinkled, his bright blond hair grew past his earlobes. Slowly he began to look more and more like the young Californian or Floridian or some other such warm-state person she was sure he was.

Maybe it was the blond hair on his ankles. Maybe it was the way he pretended to listen but didn't, as if the office were something that existed only when the surf wasn't up. More than once she'd caught him. One time she was twenty minutes into her parents' bickerings, the Saturday afternoon rows, and her mother, frustrated with what she called Cynthia's father "grabbing" her in public, that particular time on the escalator at Lazarus when she went straight home and machine-stitched shut the fly on nearly every pair of his pants. Cynthia was describing the look on her mother's face while she was stitching, both hands flat on the machine; how the trace of crows' feet about her eyes reddened slightly, like skin after a hot bath; how her lips pressed into a line so straight you could use it in geometry class. And also how her father, in retaliation, strutted around the house for days in his underwear; on the last day, before her mother gave in, how he watered the begonias in the backyard wearing a violet T-shirt and pink boxer shorts—smiling like he had just won the US Open.

Cynthia was saying all this in rather a quick, clipped manner when she noticed Beebe out of the corner of her eye looking out of the corner of his eye at something else, something not in the room: a dream he was conjuring up, right there amongst the vinyl chairs, a dream that had nothing to do with the oak furniture or the diplomas or the beard he was now unsuccessfully trying to grow, but one that unmistakably, the more she looked, had to do with her.

He was fantasizing, she could tell, about the boardwalk at Ocean City, about the backless sundress she'd told him about the week before. The opening slipped just below the curve in her lower back, the cotton a pink as soft as the inside of seashells, barely distinguishable from her own skin, tender from three days at the beach. In his fantasy, Beebe was wearing a white T-shirt, khakis, and—though she could not know for sure—bikinis the slightest shade of peach. They were strolling between couples in shorts, men in tuxes, a gang of five twelve-year-olds spitting on the slats in time to each step, and an old woman in a purple, low-cut dress, eating cotton candy by herself.

Of course, in his fantasy, Beebe was oblivious to everything but her. He was fiddling too much with the strap of her sundress, rolling the inch width of material between forefinger and thumb while they laughed about Cynthia, her crazy parents, the first time she told him that god-awful tale about her mother and the sewing machine. When he slipped his fingers slowly down her back, just inside the edge of material, then, at her waist his whole hand in and around, his middle finger at the indent of her belly button, his pinkie hooked in the elastic of her underwear, he was saying, *Yes, yes, yes, all mothers were a bit crazy with the sewing machine, weren't they? His had once run the needle clean through her finger. Like a miniature Rorschach. The blood on the cloth. Of course, I didn't think that at the time; I was young,* then slipped back into his office, into his vinyl chair, squinted for the first time in a month, and looked straight over Cynthia's left shoulder.

"And you, how did you feel about all this?"

She wanted to say that she loved the shrill whistling of the boys as she pushed the straps off her shoulders, let the dress inch down, hang a minute at her nipples, a minute at her waist, the cloth swishing against her thighs until she stepped out of the little pile of dress, sauntered over to a man selling caramel apples: $3.50 apiece.

But she knew this was not what he meant. Instead, she decided to cry and not stop until he put one moist palm on her shoulder.

The next session was better. This time when he looked away, they got all the way to the scene with the Ferris wheel: she straddling him, the teens in the chair below chanting, *Now, now, now....* That was in the middle of the story about Roger, her first boyfriend: how he'd drawn a black magic-markered arrow on the left cheek of his buttocks and printed KISS MY in blue. She'd been embarrassed to tell her father, but had felt obligated; later she cringed when she heard him laughing at a party at their house, his words slurring, KSHMY... .

Sometimes she made things up just to make Beebe laugh, just to remind him that they were, after all, about the same age, that one of his other patients had once, Cynthia was sure, mistaken her for his wife, that time at The Garage Club, dancing. And though they didn't make him laugh much, these were the stories he believed: the day her father accidentally ran over her dog, the time she threw up at her junior prom, the weeks she couldn't begin to get out of bed.

It bothered Cynthia that Beebe never told her about himself, that he sat, legs crossed, right foot tapping, as if he were only doing some job, as if it were right, after all, that she should be springing for these little tête-à-têtes, fifty minutes of indulgence. Yet she could tell that he enjoyed them too, nodding slightly at her details and, every so often, blushing—a pale line at the edge of his high cheekbones.

* * *

The second time he came to her apartment, he dressed like a salesman: brown leisure suit, encyclopedias in his briefcase. He stayed an hour and a half and took back his glasses.

Some Tuesdays, Cynthia did not go into the office. She dialed the number and moaned slightly until the receptionist clicked the switch hook, the dial tone like the ocean of a shell in her ear.

Some Tuesdays, she told him about other men to make him jealous, about her father entering her for the first time three days before her thirteenth birthday, the shadow on his face. After that, Beebe left the hour following her session open, let her curl up in the armchair and list her ten favorite shades of pink while he nodded *Yes, yes, yes* to the hum of the air conditioner.

Days like this she dreamed everyone wore flannel and was kind.

* * *

In the department store where she worked, people she thought were dead came to see her: her great Aunt Mattie, her high school Biology teacher, that boy who went away to the Marines. They brought her chocolate-covered cherries and fuchsia daisies, told her tales of love and war so magnificent she could not tell which were true, which were coming attractions at the local matinee. Their voices wove between racks of jeans and fake furs with the soft *puph-puph* of a cat on tile. She loved how her friends held her hand and stroked her hair, reaching carefully, so carefully across the counter. In turn, she showed them the latest in soft leather and new shades of lipstick. She looked the other way as they slipped gold crucifixes, digital watches, and packs of cigarettes into purses, into pockets of oversized coats.

Sometimes she saw Beebe on the escalator, a tan rain hat shadowing his eyes, strands of blond sticking out here, there. He only came to her register once. He tapped his fingers impatiently as she rang up each item twice: mint-green socks, tobacco, a plaid beach towel. When she handed him the receipt and looked at his face, the color of his eyes had changed.

After that he showed up on her doorstep often: a plumber, wrench in hand, ready to fix the faucet she'd complained about to her landlords; a poll-taker, scrawling her name on the top of some form. Once he wanted to borrow some flour, something she didn't think people did anymore. Ever.

They never talked about these meetings, even after, when he locked the office door automatically, doubled the frequency of her sessions. Now on the days she worked, she hid in the dressing room for hours, tracing the shape of her breasts. Sometimes she came to his office on the wrong day, just to sit in the waiting room, just to wait.

She wanted everyone to look like a housewife; they didn't. There were women in his waiting room with violet eye shadow, with hair shiny as cellophane. There was a man, younger than she, who rolled a pencil between his fingers, clicked his tongue as he worked a crossword puzzle, the same puzzle every Thursday, the first word across *betwixt*. Mondays at 3:00 a nun in her twenties sat in the second chair from the door, her head lowered, her skin so smooth and clean, Cynthia wanted to touch her, run a finger across her forehead, along the edge of the black cloth holding her hair.

Once she went to the office on Friday and saw her father. He was ten years younger and wore a maroon suit with a tie that didn't match. When she leaned across the vinyl chair to tell him, he kissed her.

They all kissed her: the boy with spiked hair reading *The New Yorker;* the girl with a jeans skirt slit to her thighs; the receptionist with slim hips, and Beebe, on the floor of the waiting room, stroking her hair softly, so softly. She told them everything she knew about her life and more.

The next time she went to his office, Beebe was old. His voice shook like a great uncle's, like waves above a drowning swimmer. He traced her ear with his tongue, whispered, *You are well. You should go now. You must go.*

After that she doubled her shift at the department store. She took up pottery from a man with a beard thick as seaweed. When she ordered pizza with anchovies, it was not Beebe who delivered it, but a guy named Bruce, a guy with thongs that snapped when he walked, a guy just up from Miami, trying to make ends meet. She missed the way the orange uniform hung loosely on Beebe's shoulders, how he unbuttoned one button at a time between bites of cheese.

Still, she saw his picture everywhere: on a cigarette billboard off the Interstate, as a contestant on "The Price Is Right," and even on an envelope labeled "You May Have Already Won $1,000,000." She heard him on the radio *you are well* in the middle of her favorite song *you must go*, at noon *go* on the local news. In the A&P, he shopped in the next aisle over, checking the price of aspirin, weighing tomatoes while she watched from behind a display of cheese twists. When she walked toward him, he turned and slowly pushed his cart toward the canned goods.

Once, on the outskirts of town, he pumped gas for her at a Citgo. But when he saw who she was, he looked away and charged her 50 cents extra, refused to check under her hood. Even at her bank, where she waited for him patiently, he put up the *Next Teller, Please* sign, counted someone else's money, not hers.

It was not until October, after her phone calls, after her unanswered letters to him, not until the leaves, bright as fingerpaints, twirled easiest, that he came to her, his footsteps clicking up the front walk, a Jehovah's Witness on each side.

They arrived on a day she skipped work, a morning she was barely awake. She saw them from the kitchen window and stopped stirring sugar into her coffee; she forgot the cream altogether. There were three of them, Beebe and a man and woman in their thirties, black books in their hands. She knew they would stop at her door. When they knocked, she pulled the sash of her robe tighter and unlocked the dead bolt.

They did not understand her. They sipped coffee from her clay teacups, sighed. In unison, alone, they asked again and again, *Didn't she want to trust, find peace? Didn't she want to be happy, to live forever?*

When she put her head on his shoulder, Beebe smoothed her hair automatically. The woman beside him ran a hand down Cynthia's back; the other man patted her arm and held out a handkerchief. *No, no, no,* she whispered, until even she could not hear what she was saying.

Seagulls

"The birds sound like a dog toy, squeaking." This is what she is thinking, sprawled in the backyard on a new lawn chair, face down toward the Indiana ground. She has never had a dog. The plastic strips curve out slightly with her breasts and stomach. She imagines, although she has always hated it, that this is the beach, that the schoolchildren stumbling along sidewalks have gotten lost, confused by their rumpled uniforms, and are coming, all of them, to her porch for cocktails and cheese curls the size of snails. The youngest one with the grey shell is her husband and doesn't like her in shorts, and besides, their dog, which is as small as a large-mouthed bass, has eaten all the garlic and is excessively talkative, not to mention that, as always, the tide is coming, coming, coming.

I know, of course, that the woman is I, even as I walk up in my uniform, trying to get the sand out from between my toes. But when has she ever recognized her own petticoat, uneven beneath the hem, or the dog in my voice? To her I am the yellowest line of sun when the lids are closed. And to you?

Come. There are popsicles in the icebox and margaritas in the glasses. And what better place than such pink sand to sip and love before my husband appears, and we shall, at high tide, have to bury the dog?

Dog Days

WHEN RITA RETURNED HOME from college for spring break, it was much quieter. No yip-yip-yapping at her heels. No scratching of dog nails across the linoleum floor. Her parents offered her a Diet Coke. When she asked about her Dachshunds, they told her, in an off-handed manner, that last month just before they flew to Cancun, they had had to put them to sleep. Then they asked if she'd like some carrot sticks.

The male, Hansel, had been blind, bumping into the sliding porch door at least three times a day. Undaunted, he'd turn circles and try again. His shaggy hair was always getting tangled with her mother's marigolds, which he had the bad habit of grabbing in his teeth and shaking. The shorthaired Gretel (of course) was overweight and waddled. Her belly skimmed the backyard grass and sometimes scraped the sidewalk. In the winter when she bounced through the snow, only her tail would show.

Half a semester and Rita would be out on her own. She'd been promised a summer job at the SPCA and had already checked out apartments that allowed pets. Over Christmas, when Rita had taken her dogs to the vets, she was told that, with care, they would live another eight years.

Rita thought of this later as she munched celery on the back porch. It was just too quiet to read the library book on poodle grooming. Her parents were off playing racket ball, and she couldn't help but automatically reach out her hand to pet both dogs, usually at these times, on her lap.

When her parents didn't return by 3:00 (probably having cocktails at the club), Rita took a jog around the neighborhood. Tulips were just beginning to bloom, and she counted eighty-six in a ten-block radius. All exactly the same shade of yellow—somewhere between corn and squash—they spruced up front-door walkways and lined wrought-iron fences. At a corner yard, without slowing down, she plucked two tulips and clenched them tightly in her fist.

Out of breath, she kept running, circles of sweat spreading on her tank top. When she got to the end of the development, and there were no more ranch houses and two-story colonials, she turned left and continued on toward the park, her lungs heaving. Near the entrance, a pregnant woman pushed two toddlers on the baby swings. A Great Dane, leashed to the slide, panted loudly. In the soccer field, a teenager threw a Frisbee for his Black Lab.

Rita let a tulip petal drop and kept running. She circled around the picnic tables and headed for the bike trail, a converted train track that wound through the woods. She let another petal drop. When she approached the middle-aged cyclist with his Schnauzer in a bike trailer, she tore off two more petals but didn't slow her gait.

Now her breath was coming in stops and starts, and—ripping petals as she went—she forced herself to keep going by reciting breeds in alphabetical order: *Affenpinscher, Airedale, Akitas, Afghan Hound, Beagle.* The breeze picked up, cooling her. *Border Collie, Basset Hound, Bloodhound.* She could smell it coming. *Boston Terrier, Boxer, Bulldog, Chihuahua.* The elms began to sway. *Chow Chow, Cocker Spaniel, Collie*—each syllable in time with her steps.

Dachshund, Dalmatian, Doberman Pinscher. It was then she turned again, this time off the pavement and into the woods, dropping the bald stalks behind her minutes before the rain began to pour.

Birthday Cake

SHE WAS NINETY-THREE AND had nineteen nine-inch-diameter chocolate birthday cakes from Bill Knapp's restaurant in her basement freezer. How could she say no? They were a free gift, no coupon necessary. Each cake came with a sixteen-year-old waitress smiling straight rows of braces, with a balding manager clapping chapped hands to that tune everyone loved. (Except her, the ditty going round and round her brain and into her dreams, waking her at 3:00 am. Alone.) Each came with her son and his family, who brought her every year in their Dodge Caravan, even in blizzards.

The restaurant's parking lot was always plowed. Inside, the January sun glistened off the vinyl booths, off the menus in large print. Still, the type was getting hard to read, even with her bifocals. The last several years, she had had to hand the laminated list over to Howard and ask him to read in his lawyer-like voice. She was sure he had practiced one winter when he was laid off from the office and watched the soaps for three months until a cousin got him on in the next town over. (What exactly did he do there? She couldn't remember, but it must be something important.) Even then he took her out and read the menu aloud. He was a good son. She had brought him up well.

Of course, she knew each appetizer, entrée, and dessert by heart and always ordered Salisbury steak and "homemade" mashed potatoes (not as good as hers) with a side salad. That was not the point. It was nice to hear him read like that, the way she had read so many Uncle Wiggily stories before tucking him in at night, then, such a brief time later it seemed, to Howie and Ben (both named after her dear husband, rest his soul). They, too, were good to her. Miriam and the boys (who weren't so little anymore, now were they?), they all made time. Goodness knows, it wasn't easy with boys these days and all their *this* and *that's*. They even dressed up (Howard would never let them wear jeans for this) and brought photos of their latest girlfriends though they claimed she was still their best girl. The cake, of course, came with all this, candles and song included. The boys sang harmony, the way they'd learned in Glee Club. Howard brought his camera.

The restaurant was family-owned and operated, a nice place—clean, close, and affordable. They knew her there by name. She had taught the wife's sister in her eighth-grade class and back before all that Nixon craziness was a den mother to two of her brothers. (What were their names?) The owner or his wife always made a point of coming over. They'd kiss her on the cheek and shake Howard's hand. The wife was a bit dowdy, it's true, but what a personality. She knew all kinds of stories about the old school before it was torn down for the fancy schmancy one where the boys went now. My, how they'd all laugh. Howard nearly burst a seam. Miriam would pat her on the back, and they'd both giggle like girls. Even the boys smirked, looking back and forth at all of them.

With all this, how could she complain or turn down the double-layers heaped with icing? Each time, her family insisted that a waitress box up the "free birthday gift" and have her take it home for later. "It is, after all, your birthday," Howard would explain, "and you are the only one who can afford the calories. Besides, the roses remind me of the ones you used to grow." And he was right there. She was the thinnest by fifty pounds and still had her figure. And the sugar blooms did, in a strange way, look like the Rosa New Days she had coaxed into life. How she missed those days in the garden with her Howard when they were first married, long before the arthritis and the blood clots in his legs. She'd bring him unsweetened ice tea in the late afternoon and sometimes fresh scones. She'd had glasses with yellow buds twined around the lip and a butter dish shaped like a rose. They'd sit together under the oak, their knees dirty from digging. They'd raise their glasses and cheer the day.

Not like this restaurant. Not like this cake. Her husband had hated the sight of the cakes (too much goo), but she had talked him into keeping her secret ("It means so much to the kids"), and he obliged her. Now, these last ten years, it was only her secret to keep. But not for long. She smiled to think of it.

Nine-inch-diameter chocolate cakes. Later, when he found them, Howard Jr. would be pleased. The cakes were, of course, arranged neatly, each in its own square box, marked with the year, the first when Howard's Howie was just a tot; the last would arrive in about an hour. She would bring the pastry box home from the restaurant in a white plastic bag, take it out carefully, and date the box with one of those fat magic markers she kept in the kitchen. The basement light would flicker as she descended the stairs; the furnace would hum more loudly. She liked the noises of the house, finding them familiar, comforting. She would miss that, even the mustiness of the cellar. She'd look around at the thirty-year-old Maytag, the clothes ironed and hung, the Christmas ornaments in storage, and the extra freezer. Finally, she'd take the cake box, tuck it tightly in its waiting space, and close the freezer lid for the last time.

Howard could serve them after the funeral. There was bound to be a crowd, and Miriam had so much else to prepare. Surely the owner's wife (what was her name?) made good cakes, just a little too sweet perhaps.

They froze well. She had held out for this last one. An even twenty, now that's something you could be proud about. No one could say she wasn't prepared. It would be her "birthday gift" to them.

She was so tired. She waited by the door. Howard would be there soon. She could see the lights of the Caravan approaching. The weatherman was calling for a blizzard. It was going to be a big one. She prayed the electricity would hold.

Lost

AT FIRST WE THINK she is a he in drag—late fifties, large chest, thick legs, bouffant hairdo, heavy makeup. During the concert intermission, she walks past our seats awkwardly in high heels, pointing at the floor and mumbling. "She's lost something," I say to my daughter, who dutifully writes in the small striped notebook she carries everywhere. "I don't think she can see clearly."

"How do you spell *contact*?" my daughter whispers, her 20/20's focused on her depiction of the event. Slowly, the orchestra begins again to take their seats. My daughter's letters are careful, large. Like a polite child, she stares only at what she's writing.

When I blink and pause too long, she erases her scenario. There is little left on the nub of her pencil. Pink flecks dot her skirt. She brushes them to the floor. By this time, those at the end of our row are standing, looking between seats and along the aisle. The woman with the bouffant is saying in a definitely high-pitched feminine voice, "Yes, I think it was around here," an usher has come out with a flashlight to shine across the burgundy carpet, and the violins tune up.

"A diamond," my daughter explains and begins a new story. The week before we searched our house endlessly for my lost stone, trying to catch the gleam with her Girl Scout flashlight. Together, while listening to *Peter and the Wolf,* we emptied the vacuum cleaner and sifted through dirt, dust, and chewed-up rubber bands and tissues. We swept the bathroom floor. We crawled on hands and knees, feeling for something other than toothpaste tops and Q-Tips. At the end, the gold setting on my finger stayed empty, lost without its symbol. My daughter wrote three pages in her notebook and drew a picture. Now, she flips back to check the spelling of *diamond* and how many minutes I cried. The oboists, tuning up, accompany her movements.

I stand to join the others in their search—of what I don't know. My daughter continues scribbling her new narrative, adding, I imagine, the details she loves: the reflection of light on chandeliers, the slight creak of theatre seats, the growing murmur of patron voices. Strangers gathered like this, one by one, the summer we lost my daughter at the beach. Within those eternal fifteen minutes, a teenager began searching on her bike, a mother with twins called the police on her cell phone, and an elderly couple collecting shells rushed off to get their car. My daughter, at six and just starting to write, was a mile down the sand, examining jelly fish, describing, in her own makeshift spelling, their dangerous invisible skin. For weeks after, I had trouble breathing.

Now the conductor re-appears and bows to the audience. Obediently, the usher vanishes; the other women in my row apologetically sit down. For a second before the music resumes, it is just the bouffant woman and I, shifting hesitantly on our tired feet, waiting as long as possible. We are lost together, she and I, hoping the other will point the correct direction. Except for the conductor, we stand alone in the darkening auditorium. The baton is high in the air, the haunting note of a single flute upon us as I finally slump down next to my daughter. Abandoned, the woman turns to me, opens her bright-lipsticked mouth in a sorrowful smile, and exposes the gap. Her left bicuspid is missing, the same one my daughter placed under her pillow the night before. While the rest of the Wind section joins in, my daughter turns to a blank page, begins again.

Soldier Girl

Number One Girl

WHEN THEY RESCUED ME, it was like, you know, the Great American Show: helicopters swooping in, tons of explosions, soldiers screaming, "Go, go, go!"

At least that's what was on TV—not the reality kind. In my world, I was hiding beneath the covers. The Iraqi military was long gone. Someone was shouting my name. Did you see that part? My answer was in all the sound clips. It's the title of my book, but don't confuse that with the movie; that made-for-TV thing wasn't how I saw it either.

I admit there's some things I don't remember. My dad keeps telling everyone there's no amnesia, but there's nightmares and still lots of pain, so that all gets mixed together. There wasn't knife and bullet wounds like they said at first. And I didn't kill nobody at the capture. My M-16 jammed up good. There's other things I don't want to talk about. A broken arm, a broken thigh, a dislocated shoulder from the accident—that's enough without adding what didn't happen. I don't remember any black-clad guys slapping me around at the hospital like the lawyer who helped me said. I guess it could have been when I was asleep, but why would they do that? My mom said the hospital staff donated blood. The nurse was real nice, too.

And it didn't stop later when I went home—the being nice part. Folks was just getting going. Lots of parades and gifts and medals. But it was too much and all the time. Nobody needs thousands of stuffed animals and flowers. I mean, I'm glad they was thinking of me, but I didn't do nothing real brave. Not like lots of others.

That part about the photos and Flynt—I don't want to talk about that either.

I just want to be left alone. Not that I'm not grateful; it's just I'm not good at this talking in public stuff. The TV folks promised they'd keep most of what I said, but they still added their part. The next words is straight from my gut, though, so listen good. You can believe them, unlike a lot of other stuff out there. What I really want to say is, "I wish you would all just stop talking about me."

Last Place and Counting

Yea, I'm also from West Virginia, but I'm the other one, the one you don't like. I felt kinda weird about the photos and what we were doing, sure, but I was ordered by persons in my higher chain of command. I don't regret it. You're supposed to do what you're told. And you're supposed to smile in pictures. And you're not supposed to be nice to prisoners. How else are you gonna get them to talk? Like I said before, the actions were for psy-op reasons, and the reasons worked. We were doing what we were told, and the outcome was what they wanted. They'd come back and they'd look at the pictures, and they'd state, "Oh, that's a good tactic, keep it up. That's working. Keep doing it. It's getting what we need." We were instructed to do this and that. I stick by what I said on TV. You've heard it before, so why is everyone asking the same questions?

I just want to have my baby and then be done with the rest of it. It's not like we laid in bed one night and thought, "Oh, I want to do this tomorrow. Let's do this." We didn't think of it. Something would come up, and an MI would say. "Make sure so-and-so was ready. Make sure they were softened up and weak." What else are you supposed to do? Disobey a direct order?

Then you get it for that.

And there were worse things, too. I don't want to talk about those either. I've said enough and you've seen enough. The whole world has. That photo with me pointing is everywhere—don't think I'm proud about that cigarette, either. I'm not telling kids they should smoke. Don't lay that on me.

And don't ask me about Graner. He's a user. What I said to the court-room artist stands, "Don't forget the horns and the pitchfork."

I'm sorry? That's what you want to hear, right? Ok, I'll say it, but you should talk to the guys who gave the orders. And stop talking about me. I wish you would all just stop talking about me.

Bedtime Prayers

I.

EACH NIGHT, MY DAUGHTER prays for Mr. Docker, Iraq War hero, lauded for weeks in the local paper, the parish proud of its soldier. At her school, my daughter penned him careful letters, her third-grade script girlish and hopeful. She licked stamps in his honor and crossed herself for his safe return. When he came home ten months later, no body parts missing, he presented each student with a flag and patted them tenderly on their heads. Then, he resumed his pre-war duties, sweeping dirt away from their slightly scuffed shoes. He'd pause to tell jokes in the hallway or laugh at theirs.

Each night, my daughter prays for Mr. Docker, alone in his cell. "He touched girls' private parts," my six-year-old son explains. We nod and look down, knowing what we now know, what we cannot explain, that it was his own daughter. That it happened for years. Before the war. And after.

"All our children were safe at all times," the principal writes in the emergency letter when the news first breaks, "The accused, of course, is permanently dismissed."

We do not recognize the new photo in the paper. (My children argue it is not the same man. "See how unsmiling his mouth is," they point out. "Look at the dark eyes." "Where is the uniform and the medals?")

My daughters' prayers remain the same. We are the ones who cannot sleep.

II.

And also for Mr. Carl, the Sunday School teacher who never came back, won't answer their letters. He is not in Iraq, but in the next town over, out of work, despondent, his telephone bill unpaid, the wires disconnected.

Every day after school, my son and daughter check our mailbox, waiting for the explanation of his words, he who taught them tales of the prodigal and the young rich man. "Why doesn't he answer?" they ask after the birthday card, after the Christmas card, after the please-write-back letters, after the we-miss-you-what-happened? notes.

They send their pennies and dimes. They send their crayoned pictures. In one, he is giving them a hug with his large, comforting arms. In another, he waves an American flag and holds the cross of Jesus. In a third, he is reciting the Creed. There is only enough room in the cartoon-like balloon above his head for my son to write, "I believe in…." "The rest," my daughter explains, "he can finish for himself."

III.

My son and daughter pray for us. I hear them after lights out, after my husband and I have slipped into our own beds, exhausted from the world in which we live. Their hushed voices rise up through the roof, tangle for a moment in the trees, then break free.

That's what I tell myself, starting my own prayers, naming all the names, listing them in my head in one long nightly epistle, my script as heavy as incense clouding up a room, with nowhere—within our four man-made walls—to go.

Communion of the Saints

BACK IN THE WOODS. Each Sunday. Sometimes on Wednesdays for the healing service. At All Saints, we gather together at the log-hewn communion rail. I hold a small candle for the shepherdess Genevieve and sing in my off-key alto "This Little Light of Mine," so the Devil won't blow his harsh breath. Anthony of the Desert joins in by ringing his bell and scaring away the satanic. Agatha, patroness of bellfounders, her flat chest still bleeding from her mastectomy, huddles close to protect me from drafts. Her veil smokes slightly from the lava of this year's earthquakes. Its scent entwines the incense. I curve my aging knuckles into a roof over the vulnerable candle flame. In this country church, we worship together—all saints and sinners—shoulder-to-shoulder, bent knee to bent knee.

Genevieve brings with her the Syrian shepherd Simeon, down from his sixty-foot prayer pillar for this his one consistent meal: body and blood. I know they are all ravenous. They have never tasted mutton though they must have dreamed of sheep, ox, or hog tied on a spit and roasting. (I do. Like Anthony, I bear the lusty emblem of pig.) Still, they wait meekly and hold out their tongues with patience for the circle of sacrificed flesh. When Sister Apollonia opens her bloody mouth, there is nothing but bare gums waiting for sanctification. In preparation, I swallow my own breath in prayer.

Before us and cloaked in Spirit, the priest lifts his fingers of flame and pardons our unworthiness. He enters our lips with that one great gift we sorely need. When the heat from his vestments warms my checks, I look up again to find the cup waiting. What can I do but drink every minute of this earthly day? I taste the blood as it slips out, coats the strands of my hair, seeps into my neck's skin once blessed by Saint Blaise, then slithers its way towards my heart. This greed is even harder to confess. I take only the offered sip, then let the others obey.

The taste of skin? Peeled back from soul, betrayed by the body, sweeter than my own, yet more sorrowful. Salty with tears. And the drink unwined into blood is that liquid pulse of all those bent down beside me, pooled together and cleansed, the ultimate transfusion. There is darkness, then the warm stirring of morning sun.

The arrows of Sebastian gleam in the dim light and reflect the candle glow of flames the opposite shade of Hades. Paul Miki, with his cut-off left ear, listens for all of us, then translates the angelic chorus into Japanese. I hear them singing: my mother and uncle, father and aunt, saints Peter and Paul—and Mary. They follow my lead, or I theirs. I cannot distinguish which of us belongs to which note. We are all of us rising up in song, our voices skyward and lifting.

Wise Eugenia smiles demurely, carefully enunciating Latin. Between words, I hear my name in supplication. Saint Joan reaches over to touch my shoulder, her armor bright and burning. I look then toward Rita, patron saint of desperate causes. The gash on her forehead still bleeds, still makes me weep. She looks straight in my eyes and nods.

And all the others, too, are nodding as we rise up and walk, the blood from their stigmata dripping on the maroon of the carpet. I dab the trail discreetly with Kleenex. There beside me, offering to help, is Saint Lucy, blind these many years. Unable to see, I help her back to her pew.

Water

I WAS FIVE YEARS old when I drowned.

The day was hot, but not unbearable, and I was having fun in that way you do at grownups' parties, at first resigned to it, then surprised with the ready-made friendships with their friends' kids: a dozen children splashing walls of water in the pool; echoes of "Marco," "Polo" intertwined with laughter; beneath patio umbrellas, a half-dozen grownups sipping drinks and eating shrimp on toothpicks.

Even after I went down, I could hear them. My mother was saying something about her bridge club; my father, his pediatric practice. Some others were nodding. Someone was sneezing. Someone was telling a joke I didn't understand. The talk was muffled, the way it always is under water, but other than that, all seemed ordinary enough. Tiny pieces of barbecue chicken were bobbing around in my stomach. My abandoned glass of lemonade was out-of-reach near the shallow end—not that I needed anything else liquid. The sky was calm.

I remember clouds the shape of hearts, not the valentine kind, but blood-pumping, inside-the-body-type hearts, the kind in my older brother's Invisible Man that I wasn't supposed to touch, where you could see every organ of the body. Sometimes when he wasn't home, I went into his room, got up on a stool, and stared. The lungs looked like tiny butterfly wings made of gravel.

Before I went under, my brother was counting how many seconds he could stay beneath water. He would hold his nose with his fingers and plunge down, his hair floating up like brown seaweed. He closed his eyes tightly and puffed out his cheeks. Finally, he'd surge toward the top and a large gasp of air. First child. Older by three years. Invincible. I knew that I could do better, and I did, but I waited until his eyes were again closed, then dove toward the bottom.

I counted all the numbers that I knew, all the animals, all the colors. They floated before my closed eyes in groups: turquoise, an elephant, and the number 33; orange, an orangutan, and the number 12. I counted all the people who might love me. They swam circles together. Breaststroke. Front Crawl. Backstroke. All the strokes my mother knew. Begged me to follow them. When they started to sing, like a small group of dolphins, it was harder to hear the other children and the grownups, but their voices were there somewhere in the background, going on with whatever voices do when they are talking and not listening. After a while, they all sounded like the ocean: crashing, receding, crashing again.

When I surfaced, the crashing became echoes, then slowly faded as dreams do when you wake. I was in a cave with dangling icicles a brilliant blue the color of my mother's eyes. My body flowed into the cold wet. Where did water end and arms begin? The dark lake swirled its delicate fingerprints. My breath glowed beneath the curved rock and lit a passageway of strokes beneath low archways. A sudden current turned me over.

Then I was floating again, this time inside my mother, riding the waves of her breathing, the soft warmth. Again, the sky was calm. And she was singing. To me. Wisps of lullabies she composed in those first moments of knowing and wanting me. Her syllables cradled my name, cooed my existence. No time but the refrain of her song: constant, soothing, clear. And I was happy there in that body of water. Strong. Loved.

When I was three months shy of six, I rose up, broke from her water, and swam. My mother told me about it years later, as an afterthought, when I asked why she'd given up bridge.

A Wave Rushed Over

WHAT MEGAN LIKED MOST about the breaststroke was how it pushed her into a silent, undersurface world—then brought her back, her body surging up for a large breath and a quick clip of voices and pool noise at the YMCA. Then again. She plunged under-and-forward, then up, breath, under-and-forward; the world was crisp and clean. She was both participating in and separate from everyday life, both anonymous and known. She liked that duality.

How she understood this had less to do with logic than with the smell of chlorine and the smooth water whooshing off her shoulders. Each time her legs pushed off a wall, she descended again into that first long stroke; the lane lines blurred underneath into watery fog, and she couldn't see the other end. For a few seconds, the lanes seemed to go on into infinity. But then—her arms parting the water and pulling her forward, her head rising above to see the outer world, her frog-like legs snapping into a glide—the end moved into view. At each wall, she could stop—or turn, kick off the tile, and continue. Under-and-forward, up, breath, under-and-forward. Below the surface, the water sounded like the inside of a conch shell, like whispered dreams swirling the cochlea of her ear.

Afterwards, she jogged in the waist-high water, watching women younger than she kick side-by-side with Styrofoam boards and chat about daughters' confirmations. She might have a daughter, too. And a son. She didn't know. It had been six days since she and Todd went to the clinic for the embryo transfers, six more to go before they returned for the blood test. Inside her now were two fertilized eggs—anonymous and known—that moved when she moved, forward and back in the water. She thought she could feel them at each step and stretch of her legs and whenever the water pushed against her thighs, telling her to stop. The chances of both eggs surviving were slim, but she had the power of prayer and science as her arsenal. Even Todd would laugh at such reasoning, but she knew that deep inside her something was different. Or maybe she was becoming the same as others, entering that strange world of what it meant to be average.

Of course, she would never get there completely. She wasn't absolutely sure she wanted to. The first of six children—Catholic, obviously—she was the only one of her siblings who was childless, at least until now. She had fifteen nieces and nephews, from two months to twenty-one. All of them who could talk called her "Auntie Meg." She was the "fun" aunt, free-and-easy, not "strapped" down by a household of children. She took the older ones to concerts and the younger ones to birthday parties. She was the last-minute babysitter when Mom and the teens had plans, the one who only had a husband and couldn't possibly say no. That was her sometimes-identity.

Other times, she was the "poor big sister" who "wasn't getting any younger, after all." Sometimes they looked at her with pity; sometimes with annoyance. The next oldest, Beth, told her that as a mom, she didn't have time to chit-chat and, besides, what did they really have in common? "Your priorities are focused solely on yourself, whereas mine are centered on my family." Beth said this snidely once after Megan had called to find out what the kids wanted for their birthdays since she planned to shop after work. Baby Anthony had been screaming in the background, so Beth had hung up quickly without answering the question. What Megan remembered most was how loudly the dial tone had echoed in her ear. When she tried to tell Todd later about the episode, he laughed. "Beth's just jealous of your job. With all the babies she's had, she thinks she's the one who should be teaching the little guys at St. Joe's. But look at her; she's got a kid in college and is still at it. She's making her choices."

"Was she?" Megan wondered as she started her last lap. Beth had gotten married to that macho Italian husband of hers right out of high school. That was when she and Todd were still dating. He was an usher, and she was the matron of honor in the family's first big shebang of a wedding. Her dad was still alive and got to walk Beth down the aisle. That part was nice. Megan remembered how small Beth had looked next to his 6' 4" frame. Dad had leaned over and whispered something to her. Even now, Megan wondered what it was. For some reason, it had seemed too intimate to ask. Often Megan watched the same thing with Beth and Tony, but it was Beth leaning over to whisper to her husband. Her face always had a question on it.

Even now, Beth rarely did anything without first calling Tony at his sports store. Whenever Megan stopped there to get new goggles or a swim cap, she was bound to hear his phone ring. He'd smile and flip open his cell, "Hey, Baby, I'm here working hard." What followed was usually something like, "Yea, sure make the chicken cacciatore" or "Nah, wear the green slinky one I like." Sometimes, after he hung up, he'd look Megan straight in the eyes and ask, "So how much are you and Bethy really alike?" Each time, his dark eyebrows would rise comically, waiting for an answer. She never gave him one. Still, she took whatever discount he was offering that day.

Such family interactions were a ritual—like being Catholic and making love. Sometimes, thinking of any of it made her queasy. Lots of kids, lots of family—it all went with the territory. What choices were there? What choices had her mother had? A new kid every year? Still, when her doctor had first told Megan there were "some complications" and she might have "difficulty conceiving," she had stared at him in disbelief before bursting into tears. He had delivered all six McGinney kids. He went to the same parish; he knew what her family was like, what was expected. How could he tell her the news so calmly? She wanted to punch him in the face—that's what she wanted to do—but he looked so tired and was kind and obtuse. He had even come to her dad's funeral the year before. She didn't have the heart to reject his reassurances and box of tissues. After a few more minutes of sniffling, she had tossed her Kleenex in his trashcan, then walked briskly out of the office. When the waiting room receptionist called after her, she hadn't turned around.

Now, twelve years later, she filled her weekdays teaching stories and math problems to six-year-olds at the local parochial school. Most of the kids there already had three or four siblings. Why couldn't one of them be hers?

In the pool, she slowed to a walk. Coming up to the wall, she stretched first one calf muscle, then the other. She leaned side-to-side, feeling the tug near her rib cage. She bent halfway over at the waist, staring at her toes beneath the water's surface. At 41 and 135 pounds, she looked better than her four sisters and as good as her brother Patrick, the only boy and the baby of the family. Even he had three kids notched up and a young wife who did volunteer work on the side by fundraising for charities over the telephone. She had a headphone set and would nurse while she lectured strangers on the importance of feeding orphan children in Somalia.

Once Cassie, that's her name, had even tried to talk Megan and Todd into adopting. It was a couple of years ago at one of those large Thanksgiving dinners at her mom's house. As usual, kids were running everywhere, a Monopoly game was started in the den, a football game was blaring on the

TV in the family room, and Cassie and all four of Megan's sisters—Beth, Abby, Kathleen, and Mary—were sitting in a row on the couch nursing. Megan and Todd were clearing the dessert dishes, trying to pass relatively unnoticed from one room to the other, when Cassie, seemingly immersed in a conversation with her sister-in-laws, blurted out, "Isn't that right—you guys want kids? There's a real neat opportunity going on right now because of some flexibility in the laws. I mean it's a great thing. You might even be able to get a kid from Somalia." She turned to the other women with a knowing glance, "a real win-win situation for everyone involved, and I know you guys would be really good parents if only you had this chance."

Megan hadn't known what to say, but Todd saved her with his big smile. "Good idea, Cassie, we'll have to check that out." Somehow he'd managed to throw this out in a friendly way, while juggling four pie plates and making his way quickly to the kitchen before Megan's face could get too red. Once there, Megan immersed her hands in hot, sudsy water. The sudden sting was a strange relief from what she felt as judgment. She was the one "broken" after all. The other sisters—all fertile Myrtles—kept popping out the kids. She was tired of going to baptisms and first communions. Whenever she was introduced to her sisters' friends at these events, someone always asked, "And which kids are yours?" Even at her dad's funeral, she had to explain six times that she didn't yet have children. After Cassie's comment, in the same kitchen where Megan's mom had cooked for a family of eight, she couldn't look directly at Todd. He didn't notice. Or at least he didn't let on. She handed him each fragile dish to dry while they discussed Christmas plans at his family's.

Still, Megan kept thinking about Cassie's comment—long after the dozen family hymns sung later at the piano. This was yet another McGinney tradition. Beth's oldest, Claire, played while Megan turned the pages and all the others huddled around and sang parts. Even the babies pitched in with squeals and occasional wails. When she heard Todd's strong, clear baritone blend with Claire's careful playing, she was more than proud.

Beth's Claire was Megan's favorite of the nieces—strong, loving, independent but sweet—a lot, Megan thought, how Beth used to be. Megan missed those days when she and Beth played in the school band—she on the trumpet, Beth on the drums. And how they loved to play at the family gatherings, especially "When the Saints Come Marching In." She could still hear her dad bellowing over everyone else, "O, Lord, I want to be in that number...."

That was before. Once Dad died and Beth became a baby factory, Beth couldn't stand what she called "uncontrolled noise." "It was everywhere," she'd tried to explain once to Megan. "All I want is a little quiet and a little practicality."

Still, despite Beth's objections, her oldest daughter wanted to be a musician. Now Claire was at the state school an hour down the road, close enough so she and Megan could meet a few times a month over coffee or pizza. They had what Megan wanted with a daughter: that familiar chit-chat about music, reading, and sports (Claire had made the swim team at State), as well as Claire's occasional questions about which boy to date or drop. When Claire played the piano at these family get-togethers, Megan was certain she wanted a daughter most, maybe even one, who, like Claire, shared her hazel eyes and long fingers. For a time, all Megan's fears disappeared in the confident way Claire struck even the black keys.

It was well after midnight that Thanksgiving when Megan and Todd got home, but the hymns kept running through her head, and Megan couldn't sleep. After an hour of tossing, she got up, had a bowl of Corn Flakes, then surfed the web on their shared computer, lodged in a nook off the downstairs hallway of their modest ranch. She couldn't help but type in

Somalia and *Adoption*, then wait for the computer to begin its magic. For an hour, she clicked on one site after another. There was a lot of red tape involved, the sites all said that, but it could be done. Cassie wasn't wrong.

Megan thought of the photos of Somalian children that she had seen in magazines. All she could remember were the protruding ribs. Could she and Todd get a baby? One who was healthy? She thought of all the infants she had held, all the Baby's First Christmas ornaments she had given. That night, she dreamed Claire was playing "Rock-a-bye Baby" for the entire family when, outside the window, the Christ Child toppled from the highest branch of her mom's oldest oak.

The next morning when she mentioned Cassie's suggestion to Todd, he stared at her in disbelief. "You can't be serious," he blurted out, tugging on a Got Milk? T-shirt. "I mean, we've talked about this a million times. I want someone who looks like us. I don't want everyone pointing and saying that's the adopted kid. Jeez!" He pulled on a pair of jeans. Then a pang of conscience struck; he paused and touched her shoulder. "Don't give up now, Meg, Sweetie, OK?" And, two years ago, that was that.

"Yep, and this is this," she whispered to herself, patting her stomach twice as she climbed out of the pool. She grabbed her backpack and towel and headed to the locker room showers. No one in her family knew yet about the in vitro. She might keep it that way. The Pope didn't approve, and that meant her mother, Beth, and probably the others wouldn't either. When Megan asked Todd if he thought they'd need to mention the clinic visits in Confession, he surprised her with his vehement rebuttal. "That's none of Father Bob's business…or your family's either!"

As far as the pregnancy went, if there really was one, she and Todd were waiting to tell anyone until they knew for sure—maybe until after those first iffy months. She had explained away as romantic getaways their long weekend trips to the city. And then she had said she'd had the flu and needed a few days of rest at home. What was the point of getting her family's hopes up? Of having her mom start knitting yet another pair of booties, this time maybe two? No one else in the family had had twins. They might wonder about that, too. "One more difference," she thought, "but this one would be acceptable."

Earlier that week, Megan was back to her routine, and that felt good. Except for the implanted embryos and a bit of an upset stomach, everything was the same—morning workout, then school, then home to make dinner. Here at the Y, she saw the same women in the shower room, peeling off their wet bathing suits. Each day, she watched them from the corner of her eye. They washed their body parts carefully and in the same order. They cleaned their sagging breasts, then, without embarrassment, soaped up their pubic hair. All the while, they chatted with each other about their children and grandchildren: what they loved about them and what drove them crazy. When they noticed Megan at all, they smiled at her and called her "Dear."

Today, she took her own shower quickly, using up the last drops of her chlorine-removal shampoo. She made a mental note to buy more at Rite Aid, then pulled on her panties, hooked her matching bra, and headed into the next room for her work clothes, all pressed and hanging up in a rented locker. She had a new craft for her first-graders, and she wanted to get to school a bit early to set it up.

What Megan didn't expect was to see her niece, Claire, standing in the corner near some lockers, kicking at a piece of dried gum with her tennis shoe. She looked like she had been up all night. Her T-shirt and jeans were rumpled, and her mascara smeared. And she was supposed to be an hour away at school. But here she was, and she was reaching out her arms to Megan.

It didn't matter that Megan was barefoot and in her underwear, or that her hair was still dripping. She ran toward Claire. "Auntie Meg," Claire began, her voice breaking, "You've got to swear that you'll never, ever tell my mom. I didn't have any choice."

In the morning light of the locker room, her arms stretching out toward this niece she loved like a daughter, Megan nearly tripped over the edge of a bench. Grabbing onto a locker handle, she tried to steady herself. She could almost see the child bobbing rhythmically in amniotic fluid, the girl's eyes—soon-to-be hazel—waiting for a mother's face. For hers? And then the unborn child was swimming against the current that rushed toward them, her small hands all that showed above increasingly violent waves.

Megan stopped herself from gasping and took a deep breath. She thought of Todd's hopes, her mother's expectations, her sister's horror. Then she looked again at Claire's thin, waiting arms. A wave of nausea rushed over her as she hugged her niece and let her cry.

Mom Learns of Son's Death Via Voice Mail

Omaha, Nebraska

July 11, 2003

EXPECTING A TELEMARKETER, OR the next-door-neighbor's gossip, or even her son's monotone *hi-whatcha-up-to?* filtering into the kitchen air from that metal message machine he gave her last Christmas, she hears instead the tangled wires of evening spark, ignite, light up the after-work monotony of a Friday exploding into *that* day, *that* message.

After the beep was not made for this, the officer on the other end too tired to keep dialing those same-old numbers for another mother hysterical with grief. The blank door was worse: that waiting before the knock, that never-arriving courage they were supposed to hand out with gun and badge.

If he could keep those faces anonymous, the death and tears typed in Times Regular 12-point across a screen far from their address, from her anger, from those same eyes brimming with questions he could only answer with nods, with fill-in-the-blank forms buried later in some slim folder. If only he could care beyond his daily backlog of pain piled so sloppily on the left corner of a desk that he wanted to leave by 5:00 p.m. just once.

What She Hears

Third

FROM THE FOG OF anesthesia, she hears it faintly, "It doesn't look good."
It is the nurses, Callie supposes, whispering to each other, shaking their
heads and sighing. She can't open her eyes, and her head still spins with
the sleep of medicine. The words hover, haunting the sterile room. It is
about her baby. Soon they bring her (yes, a daughter), just-washed and
fragile. Callie's own eyes are opened now, and the little one grabs at her
finger before those same nurses rush off the swaddled child. The clouds of
anesthesia again whirl her thoughts, and she thinks she hears helicopters
flying her sore body away. But it is her daughter they are taking. She is up in
the real clouds, heading for help, for someplace where they'll do more than
whisper, "It doesn't look good" beside a mother they think is still under the
sound of an intravenous drip.

First

From the beginning, the nurses cite, "Advanced Maternal Age," shoot Callie
a double take when she explains this is her first. Their practiced voices organize disasters. They hand her Xeroxed sheets with statistics; tell her what
she can and can't eat. They recite off-limit medications and look bewil-
dered when she claims this as her only pregnancy, the first time she's tried

to conceive. Like old-time typewriters clacking out obituaries, their words echo in her over-forty brain.

Later, at the Lamaze classes at the Catholic hospital, teens a third of her age sit cross-legged in midriffs. They stretch their non-varicose-vein legs easily. Half wear crosses above necklines plunging to not-yet-developed chests. They chatter about boyfriends and upcoming concerts. Some brought their mothers to coach them; some, grandmothers. Callie is the only one with a husband who isn't working second shift. When the session begins with prayer, she keeps her eyes open but crosses herself, and then crosses down to her navel.

Second

When the doctor slices open Callie's stomach and lifts out the barely breathing child, it is St. Patrick's Day. The bars are filled with happy drunks, raising their pints for luck. The hospital, however, is short-staffed. At the nurses' station, a cardboard leprechaun hangs crookedly. Without Saran Wrap, green-frosted cake grows stale. In plastic black pots, fake gold shimmers under artificial lights. No one has time to notice. The emergency room bustles with nurses wearing shamrock-print uniforms. Tired medics rush between drunk-driving victims and fight participants. It isn't a party and will only get worse. If Cassie were conscious, she would wish for a glass of Guinness. She would sing with the piped-in recording of "Danny Boy."

Fourth

"It will take a miracle," the nuns murmur, and they pray a holy span of three days, remembering to recite Jonah's emergence from the whale and Christ's descent into Hell. Even medicated, Callie can hear the click of their prayer beads at the side of her hospital bed.

Fifth

Eve could have used St. Patrick in Eden to drive the serpent out. Or to hold her hand at that first painful birth. Timing is everything. The suddenly dead Palladius made room for Patrick's bishopship. A growing patch of clover made his Trinity explanation to the king convenient and clear. Where was the saint in the operating room that night? The child came out green; that's what the doctor on-call tells Callie later, joking about the color of the saint's day.

Sixth

Still groggy from recovery, Callie is too stunned to laugh; she waits to hear her baby cry. Her mind clouds over with rearranged minutes. When the minutes disassemble, she listens for hours. Then days. It takes the entire three days, but there it is—that cry. She recognizes it immediately.

Woman Killed at Six Flags New Orleans

July 2003

WORRIED ABOUT HER GRANDSON, she double-checked the buckle—you never know about these rides—brushing his too-long bangs from his eyes—her daughter should clip those—when the ride lurched, spun, the next metal cage colliding with the just-coifed covering of her brains. And then another with a stranger's kid, his toddler eyes helpless questions.

You can't rush such pain fast enough into emergency, into fun-gone-fireworks-haywire, but you can try to climb away from it, the way in Elysburg the man with Down syndrome skinned-the-cat on the giant beams of a Knoebel's roller coaster, afraid of the jungle-gym cage trapping him high above the amusement park lights of most children's dreams. It took hours to get him down to his other life, the one before terror, where cotton candy tasted like the joy his seventy-year-old mother held out to him like a ticket.

Like others, we send our children off on rickety rides carted from one county fairground to another. We watch our kids rise up into air thick with the stench of greasy fries and apple fritters, and we wait for that first explosion of laughter or cries cascading over the metal spokes that bring them back, then away, then back, while we question what we have done, what we were thinking.

Which was, of course, about us at that size, at Hershey Park or Dutch

Wonderland, terrified or ecstatic, leaping out to a world of glorious risk so strange we screamed to recognize ourselves and our parents, far below, just one gaping mouth really, unable to save or stop us.

A *Doll's House* Redux

BY THE TIME MY author was dead, Mother was some faint legend in our family, whispered about by Anne-Marie before she, too, passed. My father, quiet as his ledger when Mother's name was spoken, turned even more serious than usual. I was grown with children of my own, but was still "that poor girl" with two brothers and a banker father, now a wealthy man who mourned without understanding. The squirrel wife had abandoned him; the cheerful mother had shut the door.

I was only waist high when it happened, but some things you don't forget, no matter who translates the tale. When the door slammed, it echoed for years. My mother's voice settled on the furniture: "a real marriage," "the greatest miracle"—all selfishness and betrayal to a six-year-old. In my dreams, we still played hide-and-seek, her dark eyes peering out from a closet or from behind a curtain. "Emmy," she'd call, "Emily Nora, Emmy, can you see me?" I see her better now, my three little ones at my knee, my husband locked up in his office, working late into the night for Father.

After she left, we were allowed no sweets, especially not macaroons. Not ever. "They destroy teeth; they rot away your insides," Father said, but we knew it was something else, something more. Some days at the park, Anne-Marie would sneak us pastries—an apple or peach turnover—but always Father hunted for crumbs, the slightest speck evidence of our immorality. Finally, we gave up and stuck to fruit, the sugar inherent and less detectable. Now, I hire no nursemaids. Without my husband knowing, I give my own children one sweet treat a day.

I still have the toy doll and cradle from that last Christmas Mother was there. Father said that it was another example of her being a spendthrift, that all her gifts would be broken before the spring. Perhaps that's what birthed my extra care. For years, I cuddled my poor dolly throughout the day and asked Anne-Marie for an embroidered handkerchief for a miniature quilt. Even if she were bought for only a few coins, didn't my Susie-Sue deserve a good mother? She smiled at me always, never closed her blue glass eyes. She witnessed everything.

When Anne-Marie tried to throw away Bob's broken horse and trumpet, I rescued them from the trash heap, glued together the splintered pieces, and tucked them under my frilly slips in the back corner of a drawer. Somehow I even confiscated Ivar's worn holiday clothes. I snatched up the flimsy wooden sword that he had broken in a fit over Mother's departure. They also went in the drawer. Each night I prayed the same blessings Pastor Hansen murmured on Sundays. It made the water from the spring holy. The horse, trumpet, clothes, sword—all were sprinkled with wet faith.

Hidden in her gifts were the last of the fairy Christmases, the tree's tinsel and candles shimmering with love's magic. Even when Father made more money, then "lots and lots" as Mother had once hoped, what could replace her simple glow of excitement? And Father's decorations, his idea of "play," well all was one more notation to be checked off the list of expenditures, everything too costly, even hugs and kisses "excessive," moderation always next to godliness. (Or maybe it is my imagination that is excessive. She did love us, didn't she?)

Father's practicality included editing our words, mine most of all because I was a girl. I learned to stitch my syllables carefully into sentences, choosing the most appropriate topics. Even with "Auntie" Christine, I kept my lips tight and my sentiments acceptable. Though she seemed to know what it was to love, in Father's eyes her choice of partners was "beneath her," a disgust that I never fully understood but which, I knew, was somehow linked to Mother, some awful failing of morals on both their parts.

And, of course, we were never allowed to utter her husband's name, that Krogstad; the word itself brought an explosion of rage from Father and a swift hit from the belt for us. Sometimes I imagined "that unscrupulous" man, as Father called him, sneaking at night into our parlor, taking a hammer and smashing our few shiny toys, the ones he couldn't afford to buy his own children. I imagined him haggard with wild hair, howling at every destruction. (But how, then, could Auntie love him so? How could his children have gathered on his lap and giggled at his jokes the way she told us?)

And I had other questions. Who, really, was this Dr. Rank? I imagined him, dare I say, as a great and mysterious lover, bringing, with his large black cape, a dangerous joy into the household. But I was told that he had been a grand friend of Father and Mother's, that he had died soon before Mother left, and that Auntie had never cared for him. Indeed, he seemed the opposite of her work-hard-and-accomplish-much philosophy. Anne-Marie said he was "proper" and "distinguished," a "constant companion to Mr. Helmer," but once a neighbor's maid told me he was "disgustin', always talkin' 'bout death and takin' no pity on the poor."

I tried not to push. The dead were dead. The gone were gone. Some days it was hard to remember. Hadn't I heard my mother and he play the piano together, laughing? Couldn't I hear them still? Whenever I asked Auntie about the mysterious doctor, she scowled and said nothing. Eventually, I stopped asking, preferring to hear tales of Mother and her at school.

I know what you're thinking: after all that happened, would my father even let us talk to her? Although she was no longer allowed in the house, many days in the park we saw Auntie Christine with her cluster of stepchildren. They were all not much older than I, a bit ragged it's true, but gleaming with happiness, bouncing after butterflies and capturing ants. Eventually, even the youngest was an avid tree climber and waved to me from the highest limb, blowing kisses that could soar the length of the park. We were not allowed to climb trees or act so undignified, though Anne-Marie let us race with the "cousins," zigzagging among the wide maple trunks.

Still, I loved those kisses, loved Auntie Christine's embraces and her fond, sad tales of my mother. She would shake her head, sigh, smile that winsome way. In her stories, Mother seemed so much younger than she, a mere girl, as if she, too, could join in the butterfly chasing. I imagined her in the highest of limbs, wildly blowing her kisses. Sometimes I knew she was chasing me, was reaching out her arm to tag my shoulder. But always when I looked it was only Bob or Ivar, hot and panting.

They, of course, are both grown now with boys of their own, who look like them and their grandfather, my Father. I'm told I resemble my mother, but I don't see it. I laugh in front of the mirror and look for that same shine I saw in her eyes. Where is it? Remembering her ways, I jump up and down and giggle for the glass. Is she there in my voice? And then I hear my husband or children calling.

They're calling now, and so I must go. This account is much shorter than my author's and only my sparse recollections, it's true, but, then—as everyone knows—I am a woman and have nothing to say.

The Wives

Peter, Peter

KEEPS ME VERY WELL? Hell should be so orange. My hands smell of it. Bits of shell beneath my nails. I can't turn around, breathe. He yells, grumbles, sighs, "You all demand too much. This place is. . . well. . . perfect for a woman! Cozy. Close to me. It smells delicious. Still, you complain. To hear the neighbors tell, your wish is my command," and on and on. My head swells with it. Summer squash, melons, gourds mashed into casseroles beneath this lid. Children crammed in every curve. I would kill the lot of them for sky and land, an elm tree and a hill. It's then he takes my hand and pulls me out. Yes, I could fill ten pies with half his sweets, then dance that piper's jig until we'd slip and slide on seeds. Damn this life the authors willed: to want and wed a man who from a pumpkin shell would carve a wedding band.

Piper

I'll pipe that tongue or pick it clean as any pepper hot off the vine; let it peter out. You talk too much. Sleep or eat instead. With me. Peck this cheek farthest from my neck and pickle what you please. This is the place to pick. Those peas will wait. The beans and peppers wouldn't dare to wither with you on your knees.

Pan

They said you'd Never, Never Land a wife because you'd fly between adult and childhood, wishing forever upon the stars and starfish. You listen still to shells, the tinkering of bells, and clocks. Old pirate ships inside your ear. At first, a cherished trait—a boy who could create on rainy days an earth complete with sun. I married you for this. Told everyone I loved that what you'd done before was play. To worry was too hard. Sure, you and I can sew a shadow, hook a captain, but look, our bones are old. Decide what you will be. The children tell their children stories of treasures, swords, and fairies, yet don't believe. But then, do we? True, you'd rather fly than fret. To wonder what, where, how, and who is much too much. To answer why is worse. There are "adults" for that—and women, enchanted by your grin. . . .

Rabbit

You've nibbled one too many leaves from someone else's garden. The neighbors point, call you "thief"; worse yet—the children can't go to school without returning black and blue. "Your old man," the bullies taunt, "can't earn an honest living. He's damned to Hell." Are these the things you want our daughters hearing? Carrots, radishes, and beans worth more than pride? I'm weary of your crimes: McGregor leering across his fence with gun in hand; your new clothes gone. Peter, sense is not your strength. The kids dream of bullets, blood, and traps, barbed wire, stew; it's lucky if I sleep at all. This has got to stop. The Cottontails come from good stock. Is your head all ears? You'll end up in jail or—more likely—dead.

Rose

A Rose by any other name would, perhaps, smell sweeter—but not to me. Your game is Catch, Catch Can. A cheater? Maybe, but I've seen ball lights strike your bat twice and fade. You say, "A hero's always right!" From dirt and plates you've made yourself. You stare down parks. Balls enough to pitch nine innings. Still, you always rise too fast. Those Halls of Fame your "honest" living complete with curves and crowds. But me? For years you saw your Reds as green, your bat as gold. This is my league. One, two, three hundred lies you're out.

Lorre

Listen, whatever rage this is tonight can wait. Psychopaths, spies, sadists, sad-eyed villains—let's face it, some nights even you forget which one you are. Your alphabet begins and ends with *M*. Nights you pace our bedroom looking for Moto or falcons, not knowing what you want. You say you can't escape yourself: the hundred shapes you've taken, the way the caged walk or whisper. Depraved is what you dream of—on-screen and off—a hunch-back and a perfect scream your aphrodisiac.

Czar

I've heard you call yourself "The Great" and brag and brag and then berate all others. But, Peter, I've seen better.

Abelard

Your monastery stone by stone inside my skin, even bones rented now to Christ, our mother Mary. A walled-up marriage chipped wide. The Canon's crucifix sharp enough to prick, cut through and off. I your Heloise: wisp of an abbess whispering inside your walls and hallways, an echo: your absence still caught between my legs.

Petros

I swallowed your fish tales whole. They wiggled in my belly years, flicked off their scales and looked like you. Really, I want to believe. This Christ cast, caught, skinned, and cleaned your body, voice; broke your life and passed it out as meal to five thousand. The leftovers are mine. I mend your nets, watch as your food gets colder, your children old, and yet I never saw the silver with which you paid our debt to Caesar. This "savior" with all his secret tricks means more to you than me? He sends swine off cliffs, tax collectors up trees; befriends the local riff-raff. Every wine I drink was always wine, and when I walk on water, I sink. I know you and your sins. Is this one more? The cock still crowing? The lies growing from your name? Rock is what he called you. But he died.

Best Face Forward

I.

WHEN YOU HAVE IT done, Elizabeth saw on one of those daytime talk shows, the plastic surgeon cuts new slits for your ears, then tugs the skin back, up, and over. Your ability to hear remains the same. Her sixty-six-year-old mother was 2000 miles away recuperating from plastic surgery in Houston; she'd already had it done. Elizabeth learned of the surgery after-the-fact in a phone call from her sister. The time for arguing was over. Back, up, and over. Skin stretched like not-enough pie dough needing to fill the tin.

II.

Her sister's cancer was bigger than a dime and square on the lower lid of her left eye. The doctors used the word "deformed," pronouncing it carelessly in the examination room. Her mother worried about how her sister would look in new photos, and, of course, what her youngest daughter would be able to see.

Her sister was awake during the operation, aware of her husband watching her. They had splurged and gone to a hospital instead of a cut-and-burn clinic. The pathologist kept coming in and out, shaking his head. After three times, he nodded. Afterwards, they gave her the sulfa she was allergic to, and still later, when she broke out in raw rashes, a bill reduced by $5000. A good deal, overall, her sister said. After three weeks, her ability to see returned to normal.

III.

Elizabeth scanned the *Time* magazine article entitled, "When Doctors Say They're Sorry." She cut it out carefully along the lines but did not mention the piece to her sister.

IV.

After Elizabeth tried on her mother's Liz Claiborne hand-me-downs, there was nothing new to wear. Buttonholes refused to meet buttons. Hooks and eyes failed to communicate long distance to each other. Zippers, at their worst, dug into her skin and stuck. At their best, they bulged. Altogether, Elizabeth tried on ten blouses, five sweaters, eight skirts, and one pair of elastic running pants, the latter too tight for her hips. She recently had lost ten pounds.

The next day, over coffee, her mother offered to pay for breast reduction and a tummy tuck. "It could be your birthday present," she explained, stirring NutraSweet into her decaf.

V.

The daughter smoothed the size-twelve skirt she was wearing and looked away. Her ability to feel remained the same.

VI.

"An explication," Elizabeth wrote on the blackboard for her freshmen, "is the process of analyzing a poem line-by-line, and similar, in fact, to writing the poem itself." She squiggled some lines to look like text. "It also is not unlike the work of a surgeon," she explained, "evaluating, diagnosing, dissecting, amputating or augmenting where necessary." She circled the squiggles, then drew a dotted line out to the side—the way she did when diagramming sentences for Secondary Ed students. "Start by taking careful note of what makes up the whole and how it is shaped."

To avoid sneezing, she dusted the chalk off her hands, then began again. "And always look for second opinions." She nodded toward the quietest girl in the front row. Once again, she had forgotten her name, but no matter.

"Take, for instance," she continued, "the poem on 1228 of your text." While students quickly flipped the pages of their anthologies, she announced, "an over-taught piece, yes, but in this case, appropriate." She circled the room, reading slowly, articulating carefully, and eyeing up her clients.

She was good at building suspense. She knew how to milk the persona of confidence. "First, are you *our* sort of person?" she interrogated, gaze straight ahead and serious. "Do you wear a glass eye, false teeth, or a crutch?" She tugged the hair of a cheerleader who had fallen asleep so that she woke with an "Oh!" No one laughed. All eyes were on Elizabeth in her blue pantsuit and professorial face. Her sensible flats clicked drama across the tile.

"A brace or a hook, rubber breasts"—a football player and an accounting major smirked—"or a rubber crotch?" They stopped. She walked toward them, then veered suddenly away.

She took a deep breath. "Stitches to show something's missing?" She started slowly in a whisper, for she planned to continue in hushed undertones. Somehow, though, by the end of the query, her voice gained momentum and volume, the last words replaying themselves like a stuck record. "Missing, missing, missing?" She realized too late that she was shouting.

She turned away for a moment, erased the blackboard, and then faced again her waiting audience. Fully composed. Face Forward. Her ability to think remained the same.

For Real

WHENEVER HER DAUGHTER GOT up to bat, Marlene held her breath. There was usually a third grader doing jumping jacks in the outfield, Bobby LaTrobe's mother yelling to her son as he got ready to pitch, and lots of shuffling around in the dugout with all the Pineville Hospital team kids trying to see what would happen. All this was periphera. With her daughter's eyes focused and her breathing unsteady, Marlene could sense Annie's heart whooshing its own irregular exchange of *shush-ah, shush, shhhhh, sha-shush.*

Each time, the pitch seemed to hang cartoon-like in midair between ball and strike, waiting for the whim of the umpire, or a nurse just off-duty. In those seconds, Marlene watched for the first sign of Annie's decision: to swing or to wait, to try or to pass, to inhale or to exhale, to will her heart to pump normally or to let the beat swing wildly into the erratic.

What she both wanted and feared was that signal in her daughter's brain that translated, "Yes, do it!" Sometimes that happened, the bat connecting so perfectly with leather that Marlene could hear her own shout in the clack. Then her daughter would be running, dust scattered by her hand-me-down cleats, her helmet slightly askew, and her arms pushing toward home. The specifics of the game were extras. It was her daughter she watched, her thin legs and arms that she applied to baseball terminology. Of course, she cheered as well for the others, but only as melody to her daughter's harmonious heart murmur, the true music of summer that kept her own life beating.

The doctors had said it was a relatively minor defect, a small hole that might close by itself over time. It pulsed the sound of a waterfall; the louder the noise, the tinier the opening, the less risk. "And, yes, she can play sports," the pediatric cardiologist had promised. "Overall, the exercise will be good for her. Just use common sense. . . ." And then he had tugged at his stethoscope and opened the door for them to leave.

"Common sense" was a mystery to Marlene. It seemed mostly to have to do with living a normal life, defined by her husband and children as Little League in this new-to-them small town on a summer evening. Most of the parents worked at the paper mill, some at the two family-owned restaurants, and a few at the hospital as nurses or maintenance crew. Her husband, a chemist, coached their son's team, but the games often conflicted, so here she'd sit among strangers in her fold-out sports chair, as close to home plate as the fence would allow, and her daughter within yelling distance. At her side, in a somewhat tattered Notre Dame backpack, was often a stack of ungraded middle-school book reports. For these, she'd earn hot dog and hamburger money and a few extra dollars for babysitting the pre-teens condemned to summer school, all of whom, she knew, would be off later to a soccer or ballgame like this. That's what she said. What she thought when she deposited the paycheck was "Here was money for the future, her just-in-case fund for doctors in some larger city."

When, a few weeks after their move, the lit survey class had fallen in her lap, she was surprised and ambivalent. Their realtor was the principal's nephew, and he spoke in hushed tones when he told her of the office affair, a teacher's sudden dismissal, and the need-to-fill-quickly position. When her husband got his new job, she was prepared for the transition of time off before her own job hunting. She imagined getting the house in order and going for long walks with the kids that ended up at Dairy Queen. But the early morning teaching got her home by 9:30, her husband off to his slightly adjusted schedule, and free afternoons and evenings for these games. To be honest, teaching children of people she did not yet know wasn't as bad as she expected. It was early enough in the season that she'd invent their names when they elbowed their ways onto the small set of bleachers where she didn't sit. Five of them looked like the parent of her worst student. Despite the high percentage of family relatives in town, in this instance her common sense prevailed. She smiled at everyone, but stayed in her folding chair.

Except when forced not to. After weeks of avoiding it, one cloudy afternoon, purely by accident and almost after the fact, she found herself signed up for concession-stand duty. It was the bottom of the first, and her daughter was in the outfield—looking more at the clouds than the coach—when a twenty-something pregnant woman in a ketchup-stained apron came out of the Ballgame Burgers trailer asking for a "Marley something." When Marlene automatically turned her head, the woman sighed, "This is you, right? Says you're up for duty, and Sis needs a register gal. This you?" and she pointed to a sign-up sheet where Marlene's husband had sometime (who knew when?) scrawled her name.

Of course, she had to go, abandoning the unopened backpack and the folding chair, abandoning a full view of her daughter. She hoped, though, there'd be a spot to watch from the trailer, a side angle that gave her at least a glimpse of the game, of her daughter and how she was. She was a worrier; her husband told her this at least once a week, but she couldn't help but glance back twice as she followed the woman to the trailer. She waved to Annie, then pointed to the shack. Annie waved back and kicked something on the field. At the same time, the other team's runner stole second.

Inside the food trailer, an older woman with a hair net was barking chicken finger orders to Jason, a thin teen simultaneously working the fryer and rocking his hips to some inner music. His Jesus-Is–the-Great-Physician T-shirt had grease stains and a rip under one arm, but what Marlene could not help but notice first was the cast on his left foot, a cast he seemed completely unaware of as he rocked back and forth, pushing this button and that, flipping a burger on the nearby grill, and lowering the fries basket into hot grease.

The older woman, Sis, snapped, "There you are," and pointed Marlene to the cash register. "Them's the prices up there," she nodded at a faded sheet taped on the wall, "and these here are the buttons you push after each item, then at the end." With a long unpolished fingernail, she tapped first a yellow then a red button. "Think you got it?" She waited for an answer and when Marlene looked into the older woman's face, she saw she was kind after all. A few strands of gray were peeking out from under the net and falling above tired eyes. Sis swatted them away, but still waited. "Hon?" she prompted.

"Oh, yea, sure, I think," Marlene stammered, just as the next person in line ordered two hot dog meals, three soft pretzels, and a large bag of BBQ sunflower seeds. At first she tried to hurry—$2.25 for hot dog meals, $3.50 for hamburger meals, $4.25 for chicken fingers meals, Pepsi or Sierra Mist?—but the numbers got jumbled in her brain, and she'd forget the orders. *Shush-sha, ping, shush, pa*—the register echoed an irregular heart beat, and try as she could, Marlene just couldn't focus. She kept picturing school charts on how to administer CPR. "There's a nurse umping," she told herself and handed back change from a twenty to a guy in a bowling shirt.

It was better when she took a deep breath, slowed down, looked into each customer's face, and smiled first. She recognized some of them from the bleachers, and some from the grocery store. One was a student who sat in the third row back and had written a halfway decent paper on "Casey at the Bat." He tipped his ball cap. "Hey, Teach," he smiled, then ordered a grape Slushie.

The pregnant woman, Jenny Lou, handled most of the drinks, the cheese fries, the soft pretzels, the candy orders—and anything else when Marlene's line backed up. For the most part, Sis sided up with Jason on the grill, sizzling burgers and cracking jokes about the local butcher and the high school girl's track coach. Jason, it seemed, was sweet on one of the runners, at least he blushed at her name, Susie Stanley. Marlene imagined Annie at that age, working the grill at some Little League game, giggling with some boy like Jason who might break her heart. She looked again at his cast, scrawled with the names of friends. Was he the type of kid who looked for danger? Jumping off Hanging Cliff when the river was low? Or had he merely tripped at a high school race? As she rang up a bag of pretzels, she wondered how much it hurt and if he'd gone to the emergency room.

If there wasn't much of a line and she stood a few feet to the left of the register, Marlene could see the team up for bat. She caught parts of the second and third inning this way, saw Annie walked once, then later tagged out on third. She couldn't see the scoreboard, but customers kept them posted, and her heart sank when, the next time up, Annie struck out. Her daughter hung her head a bit and half-stomped back to the dugout. Marlene imagined her breath in jerks, her heart racing, and her lower lip pushed out in disappointment. Then the next batter was up and hit a triple. The kids in the dugout went ecstatic, slapping high fives and cheering with Annie in a makeshift huddle. She jumped up and down, her pigtail bobbing. The team made two runs after that, then a final out. Understandably, Marlene's line jammed up again, parents anxious to get their food and get back to the game.

She was busy then for a while, pushing buttons—*Shush-sha, ping—*

counting out bills, and grabbing cold cans of pop from the freezer. She saw their realtor, now in jeans and a Bud Light T-shirt, and laughed when he did a double take at her temporary job as cash girl. "Didn't recognize you without your house," he chuckled. "My kid is pitching now. Already struck out the neighbor boy. Won't help the cookout tomorrow." He laughed again, trying to juggle five Pepsi's, then wove his way through a group of cheering dads on his way back toward the third-base line. He, too, she noticed, avoided the bleachers, heading instead to a large half-circle of folding chairs. She thought she saw the principal in the grouping, but it was hard to distinguish him without his desk and tie. And then there were more orders.

By the time the rush was over, she was starting to get used to the smell of grease, the irregular *shush-shush* of the cash register, and the feel of sticky quarters handed to her by grade-schoolers wanting more Baggies of purple gummy bears. Her daughter's team had gone out and come back from the field, and it was the top of the fourth.

She wiped up some ice tea spilled on the counter, then inched over to the left of the register for a better view. With no one in line now, Jenny Lou joined her, her face flushed, a large circle of sweat on her protruding stomach. "My third," she smiled and patted her belly. "My first is on your daughter's team." Grabbing a piece of ice from the bin and rubbing it across her forehead, she added, "the silly kid with the crew cut—they've got him as short stop now." Marlene wondered how Jenny Lou knew Annie was her daughter, but then remembered how much she must stand out—new substitute teacher in this small town with one of the two girls on the team—her illusion of anonymity fading once again. She picked up her own piece of ice and chewed on it slowly, the sweet cold cooling the back of her throat.

She was just starting to exchange stories with this other woman, the way mothers do when they've first met, comparing funny sayings, sports scores, possible family vacations, the cost of clothes these days, or the names of pediatricians. Sis and Jason, scraping off the grill, were even joining in on the conversation. "When we were little, we used to go to that doctor on the corner of Oak," the teen shouted over the hum of the grill fan. "He'd give out sugarless bubblegum if you didn't cry." Right after, when the boy smiled wide, Marlene knew that that runner, Susie Stanley, would say "yes" when he asked her to the prom the following year.

Then Annie was up to bat again, and they were all, this whole Baseball Burgers crew, watching together, cheering her on from the trailer, calling out her name. Sis put two fingers in her mouth and whistled the loudest Marlene had ever heard. The first pitch was way over Annie's head, the second a strike, but the third a straight line, at which Annie pulled back and swung hard, the ball driving fast past third and into the outfield. Marlene was watching the other team scramble for the hit and her daughter charging pell-mell toward first. Her heart, she was sure, worked just right for once. In the rush, she didn't even see the bat, slung full force from her daughter's arm, strike the on-deck batter squarely on the side. When Jenny Lou gasped, Marlene thought she was excited for Annie. For a moment, she felt she belonged.

Then the child fell back. The nurse/umpire came running, and Marlene and Jenny Lou, faces equally shocked, bolted toward the trailer door and out to the field. By the time they got close, Annie was there too, crying hysterically, bending over her teammate until the nurse shooed her away. Jenny Lou helped her boy up as carefully as she could and huddled him close to her stomach. Another mother immediately called an ambulance.

On their way to the dugout, the boy staggered and nearly fell. Jenny Lou caught him, but called out anyway for help. From the trailer, Jason was already swinging out on crutches, a small bag of ice slung over his shoulder. He and the nurse kicked out the rest of the Pineville Hospital team and made both mother and son sit on the bench. "Give them space to breathe," Jason ordered like an adult.

The sun had just emerged from the clouds when Marlene and Annie heard the sirens. The boy was better by then, even smiling a bit with his mom, but Marlene and her daughter waited anyway behind the fence until the emergency squad had pulled up on the grass, as close as the driver could get. "Slugger," the EMS men called to the now-talking boy, "Hey, Attention Grabber," and then they winked at Annie as they walked by.

"His name is Casey," she whispered to her mother as the men helped her teammate and his mom into the squad.

After a few minutes, of course, the game went on. It always did. Sis and Jason held down the fort at Baseball Burgers. Marlene hovered near the dugout. Annie went back to first, but never made it further. The next two batters struck out. The Pineville Hospital kids returned their last time to the outfield, gave up two more runs, but still won the game. Some of the team moms cheered as usual. Some didn't. A few took their kids to the Dairy Queen afterwards to celebrate.

Marlene and Annie went straight home. They forgot the folding chair and the backpack of ungraded essays, but it didn't matter. Sis would return everything to them later that night. Marlene was sure of it. She left the porch light on.

The "boys" were still at their own game. Most likely, her husband and son would return with a whoop. They'd pull out the double-chocolate ice cream from the fridge and, between bites, would trade stories of the team's best plays.

For now, Marlene was glad for the calm. Arm in arm, she and Annie walked upstairs. At the top landing, she pulled her daughter in close under her arm, then tight up against her chest. "Your heart is really racing Mom," her daughter looked up and said. "I can hear it. For real."

Rachel Isum Robinson: Snatches and Excerpts

Rachel at Home

I'M A SOMETIMES-CINDERELLA, SURROUNDED by encrusted pots and pans, hands deep in hot water, scrubbing. My worn-out mother caters to keep the coins coming. When my father turned ill, she told me, "We'll work together, have a wonderful life." She keeps us going. I keep us going, soaking my brothers' dirty clothes, tending to my father. I'm a sometimes-Cinderella, but with suds of hard work and palms raw with what must be done in the name of father, mother, brothers, love.

Rachel Meets Robinson

When the world spins, I hum "Stardust" and "Mood Indigo"; the slight stir of Jack's sweet breath hovers near my ear. When the world fox-trots, my polished black pumps click on the clean tile of the Biltmore Hotel, all the glitter and glitz of LA twirling. How we sway in our first-date-look-at-us clothes—blue suit and ebony gown. How we dart and turn, Jack's polite hand just-so on my shoulder. I want to leap into love with each Lindy Hop, the ballroom spinning with it, my young head whirling with first glimpses of his handsome contradictions. In all my swirls of memory: UCLA, crisp white shirt, shy confidence, angry pride shimmying toward our first peck of a kiss. Under the rotating ballroom lights, Jack adjusts my adult-like fox-trimmed hat, then lightly touches my hair. We know.

Rachel Waiting

While he salutes, I rivet. While he yes-sirs, I rivet. While he petitions, while he talks back, while he insists, "No!" while he keeps battling the Army's stand-here-and-do-that-because-of-who-I say-you-are, I rivet.

Nights at Lockheed Aircraft, the other women and I fasten ourselves to the low moan of machines. Sparks flash in our eyes. We lean into the ritual of industry, hungry for roles. We secure our sweat to cockpits, energize our wills with the electricity of national cause. We manufacture patriotism and praise the dirt of hard work. At sunrise, I scrub my chapped hands and hurriedly change clothes in the university's parking lot. There, I transform back into student: because of who I am, because of who Jack is becoming. Both of us—riveted.

Rachel Still Waiting

Idleness makes absence deeper. With my father dead and my athlete-turned-lieutenant still fighting the Army, I put on the starched dress of hospitals. I learn patience, care, and how the ill need our touch as much as the well. My hands can handle both. I will not wallow in waiting. Let me ache with the daily stretch of compassion. Each finger learns by doing. The years prepare us for what we can't expect—the calluses that come with time, that prophesy the balm of a calm voice when your man strikes out, but still makes it home to hands that can ease, just a bit, the pain of the angry season.

Rachel Listens

What you can't see over the telephone wire, you hear in a voice. After his meeting with Mr. Rickey, Jack's is all exclamation. Syllables bounce from his vocal chords and across the stretched line of distance. I listen as the future tries to tightrope to my ear. I want to unbalance fear, but even joy can trip the sure step. I hold my breath, hear everything that may or may not become.

Somewhere in that other state, the secret handshake of men clasps details. My own hand trembles, then grips the receiver even tighter. Far away on the other side of the line, Jack is still talking. In his intonation, I hear "job" and "marriage." I hear how the long-held hope in our hearts may begin to materialize even outside our bodies.

Rachel Become Robinson

Ah. Look. I am. Pre-war ivory satin wraps my breath in expectation. Jack, too, gleams with it. His head tilts toward mine into our sphere of private happiness made public. Beside us, my aging mother beams. Our gift to her: a fantasia of ceremony, a regal ritual to indulge her own desires. My love and I love to see her happy. I am. We are. What will be is still becoming. We are. Joined together. Willing.

Rachel by Plane and Greyhound

Lines. Dust. Sky streaked with my sorrow. Air turned stale with hate. Daytona Beach and spring training awaiting, I don't anticipate the *White Women* sign at the New Orleans airport bathrooms. In my fur and fine hat, I don't expect the unexplained removal from the plane. And now, a day later, as we move to the back of the bus in Pensacola, what can I see outside the dirty window but despair? The world blurs by—all lines, dust, sorrow, hate. What jagged path awaits? I strain to see safety, to find even a small space where our aching feet can stand. With each bump of the bus, the future turns another corner I can't see.

Rachel in Montreal

Here strangers look us straight in the eyes, say, "Welcome" and mean it. On the field, training is rigorous but familiar; we welcome the ritual of hit, catch, and run. At each game, full-throated cheers surround and soothe us.

Along our street, so many new faces and most friendly. I turn right; I turn left, waiting to see the scowls, but here neighborhoods come complete with "neighbors"—the real kind that want you to stay. In our own home, I learn to breathe more easily. This child within me houses all that I want. We prepare—on every level—for what will be.

Rachel Back in the USA

In this new world of Dodgers, amidst the taunts and death threats, each day we write a little more of our lives. The details are hard. The sharpest syllables stick too long in our throats, won't let us swallow what we truly want: the simple pleasure of being. Slurs spike our weeks, leave welts the size of worry. Some days the jeers echo so loudly they scare any possibility of sleep. Then, even the moon can't calm me. In the dark hours, each night echoes fear. I hold my husband and child closer. Whenever and however I can, I protect home. I will not let us fail.

Rachel Content

Yet despite all this, there are joys: long bus rides with the baby; a quiet, simple meal for three; uncontained ecstasy on the ball field; and the slow change of this still surprising world. When my love runs his pigeon-toed run, our life is a round, glowing ball of hope. The future shines in the crack of his bat, in the hard-won respect that now surrounds him—with or without his glove—in bright bursts of possibilities.

Rachel Continues

Ballpark anthems and neighborhood ballads pave the way to where we are headed. Ours are not the only voices singing as we travel on. The road is full of the dark tones of bass, the brave baritone and tenor, and the constant courage of alto and soprano. It is a song we have always known, but it is free now to rise, to flow from our willing lips, to ride the breeze and the tornado over skyscrapers, shacks, tenements, and estates. Join us. Inhale deeply. Open your mouth. Wait for the words to come.

Rachel Ever Learning

We stretch and stretch—this way for Jack's Hall-of-Fame glory, this way for my morning commute, this way for Mother's herding the children toward adolescence. I stack medical facts in my overly busy brain, then stretch my arm toward my master's diploma. I stretch back toward who I've always been; I stretch forward toward who I'm still becoming.

The nation also stretches its limbs, trying to push past childishness. We all feel the necessary ache and stretch harder. When our brothers and sisters march, we march with them. It has been a long way from the ballparks to Birmingham to DC, but we continue stretching, continue moving. We will always be moving.

Rachel Mourns

First for Martin, then for Jackie, now for Jack. Despite the whirl of memory, the world is awash with blue-black loss. The jazz that once lifted me sinks to blues. Drums become my pulse; the piano sings low. O, Ella, hold me now with your knowing notes! *Ol' clickety-clack's a-echoin' back th' blues in the night. The evenin' breeze'll start the trees to cryin' and the moon'll hide its light when you get the blues in the night. Take my word, the mockingbird'll sing the saddest kind o' song, he knows things are wrong, and he's right.*

Rachel Still

Sometimes grief hangs too heavy. My heart throbs with it. My limbs refuse to move. My mouth forgets the hope of language. The world is a small, dark room closing in. And then my Sharon and David step in, dragging the light behind them. And there are other children, and in between I catch my mother's soothing voice. And behind her, I hear the stirring of so many patients, waiting, waiting for the quick clip of my nurse's shoes. And far off, growing louder, I hear the chants of all those who took a step out of sorrow when Jack stepped up to base.

Because of them, I tell myself. Because of him. Because he kept stepping up even in the hot lights of the game. Because the game isn't over yet. Because there's always another child hoping, watching, waiting for the chance to finally play.

Rachel Now

Now is the time to stop reading this story. Look instead at the young women. They are in the factories and the schools, in the grocery stores and the law offices. They are checking your pulse at the hospital. They are measuring the strength in your heart and hands. They know what is possible.

And watch the men. Follow them, too. They are crossing the busy streets. They are running the lonely marathons. They are walking the shadow-clad alleys. They are climbing the sharp cliffs. There I am.

And over there.   And here, too. Listen

       to what I am   saying through them.

Keep moving   all the way   to home.

Watching *42* at the Dollar Matinee
with My Mother

AT 84, MY MOTHER is showing her age. She hobbles into the already dark theatre to watch the movie we've previously seen separately but not together. I, recuperating from a broken foot, also am hobbling. Yet, despite the shadows and our less-than-perfect health, I easily find my place beside her—again. As the film begins, we both are caught up in Jackie Robinson's story, but silent in our own reflections. Then the camera zooms in on a cigar-smoking slightly rumpled gentleman with bushy eyebrows. My mother leans over and whispers excitedly, "He sounds just like Uncle Branch. He really does." While most of the largely senior audience sees Harrison Ford in that Midwestern second-run theatre, my mother and I see family.

We have been warming up for this ballgame movie for a while now: chatting about one of its subjects—the Robinson/Rickey partnership—for many of my 54 years, 54 years, like my mother's 84, that continue to witness needed change.

Two years earlier, while drafting a juvenile biography of Branch Rickey, I craved the familiar stories as only my mother could tell them. Bound together by the power of story and family, we spent hours on the phone. I listened as she reminisced about a man who wrote her letters, who taught her his favorite poems, who treated her to New York outings, and who took her to ballgames where, as a girl and young adult, she met such celebrities as sportscaster Red Barber, manager Leo Durocher, and comedian Jack Benny. During our phone conversations, she laughed at her great uncle's notoriously bad driving and admired his abiding faith. In between, I added my few, brief recollections: family birthday parties where, at three or four, I leaned against his shoulder a few years before his death.

Mostly, though, I learned even more deeply the tales behind baseball's "Great Experiment." With each story retold, my deep respect for the Robinsons and my great granduncle grew deeper—and so did my relationship with my mother. As we gazed up together at the silver screen, I was reminded again how stories and memories bind us together, how values are passed down through generations.

My mother first saw *42* at its grand opening at Ohio Wesleyan University, the alma mater she shared with Branch Rickey, the great uncle who made it possible for her to attend and receive her degree more than sixty years ago. Along with several family members, she sat mesmerized in that beautiful Strand Theatre, which, during my mother's college years in the late 40's, hosted reruns of *Gone with the Wind*.

Later, four hundred miles away in Pennsylvania, I heard my mother's lively narratives of the Robinson/Rickey celebration: the insights and kindness of Branch Rickey III, and—of course—scene-by-scene accounts of Brian Helgeland's cinematic retelling of baseball's "Great Experiment."

When my husband, two children, and I later sat in our own small-town crowded theatre, we, too, re-experienced through the camera's lens both our country's and our family's history. Watching the responses of my children, I witnessed once more how values travel generations. As a family, we clapped for all that has changed. And then we talked—about the need to make a difference, about the importance of continuing on toward what is most right and good.

84

Sharing that second, later viewing of *42* with my mother, I was blessed with the added commentary of her memories. We laughed, sighed, and dabbed our moist eyes together. By the flickering light of that movie's projector, we looked back and ahead. We were able to hope that the experiences passed on from one generation to the next could continue to instill change. And so, after the credits rolled and the theatre emptied, my mother and I hobbled on our weakened bodies into the afternoon sun. The day was not yet over. There were still a lifetime of stories to discuss. There were still ways to make the dark corners of the world brighter.

Exhibition

"The ability to simplify means to eliminate
the unnecessary so that the necessary may speak."
-Hans Hoffman

BRUSHING A WISP OF gray hair from her forehead, Mae applies a coil of
clay to the nude she is sculpting. With her thumbs, she smoothes and
shapes a ridge of tightened muscles across the stomach. Then she steps
away from the sculpting stage and stares. Slowly encircling the form, she
tries to memorize the various angles. There is still too much, she thinks,
that is unnecessary. She chooses a small steel scraper from her tool tray and
shaves off more clay from the waist and thighs. Then her practiced fingers,
stained red by the terra cotta clay, reshape the hanging breasts. She dips
her rounded end brush in water and better defines the cleavage. To create
the look of skin, she dabs the surface with a slightly moistened sponge,
softening the way the light hits the clay.

Two feet tall, the form will be a miniature of herself about to spring into
a dive: knees bent, calves tensed, thin arms raised and flattened against the
soft curls shoved back from the ears, toes starting to push off into whatever
lies ahead. She had first planned a more traditional pose and had finished a
sketch and fashioned a maquette of her seventy-five-year-old self draped in
silk and seated on a stool, meditatively glancing over her shoulder as if for

a great and famous artist. But once she finished these preliminaries, everything felt wrong. She didn't like to sit. She didn't own any silk. If nowhere else—she thought—she deserved the action of her imagination.

Besides, action meant change, and no matter whether she planned for it or not, change seemed to splash all about her. Better to bend her knees and prepare to spring forward. Of course, there was always the matter of losing balance while she waited. That was the risk. It had happened before. Even last week, waiting on her front porch for a ride, she had lost her footing and nearly toppled over the handrail into a pile of leaves she had raked earlier that morning. Had she instinctively prepared for her own fall by softening the ground with such bright colors?

Now, with wood ribs in hand, she scolds herself for being silly. In truth, she had been too exhausted to bag the leaves. And she had grabbed the handrail hard and righted herself successfully. There was nothing else to it. No need to tell anyone. She hadn't said a word when her ride pulled up.

With the wood ribs, she trims more clay from the muscled calves, then looks again at the slightly off-balance form of herself. What was the best way to give the illusion of motion? To suggest movement without sending the statue toppling to the floor? She scores the base and shores up the foundation with additional clay. With a metal scraper, she arches the toes a centimeter more. Was that it? She takes a wire brush and textures the clay into long blades of grass curling in the wind over the statue's heels and toes.

Again, she stands back, then reapplies the pressure of her tools. She scrapes away additional clay to better define the blades. More and more, they resemble waves. She rolls another coil. She attaches the coil with slurry then transforms it into a twirl of seaweed climbing one ankle. "Maybe," she thinks, and steps back again to look.

Her upcoming exhibit—a retrospective—is two weeks away. "Self,

Diving" will be the final piece. What she wants it to express, she is still discovering. She keeps the seaweed in place and looks again at the angle of the head. This is the last form friends and patrons will consider as they return to the ordinary world: a head slightly tucked but moving forward, a body following that determination.

Her opening sculpture is also a nude, herself at seventeen. In that one, she is kneeling, her head lowered in prayer, her palms raised in praise. If patrons were to look closely, as they should, they would see the statue has no eyes, merely large sockets where Mae has forced her thumbs to dig in. From experience, Mae knows most people will focus instead on the hands. With a metal teasing needle, she has carefully crafted each clay fingernail to point toward heaven.

Much of Mae's other work is in oils, impressionistic paintings of her travels in France or the farmlands of southern Ohio where she played as a child. Points of orange and red merge sun and fields. Lavenders and blues blend to offer up a familiar landscape of hills. But there are unexpected pieces, too. Sharp angles and incongruities: it is a different type of sculpting. With color and shadow, she can shape perception. She can adjust expectations. She can give the illusion of movement where there is none. She can soothe or surprise. Sometimes, Mae starts off trying to do the one, but ends up accomplishing the other. How long had she stood back and stared at "Prayer"? At one point, she had thought she was done, then surprised herself and rebuilt the lowered face, adhered more wet clay, and plunged her thumbs in.

The oils, also wonderfully messy, exposed the hidden. Even in the idyllic landscapes, something else lurked—a crow in the corner of the sky, the tip of a scorpion's tail descending in sand. Yet in scenes she deliberately cast as unsettling (as in a series one reviewer dubbed "Angelic Nightmares"), something good crept in. The combination of color and line surprised *and* soothed. Fear transformed into worship. How this was possible, she could only articulate with brush or chisel. Words were relegated to short titles—unpolished door-knobs to push open the meaning. The eye should do the rest.

Even so, it could be troubling to title the character studies. Those of strangers were simple enough, but the paintings or sculptures of those she loved? How to suggest duality? To recreate the real but not harm the original? She thought of the details that made up love—the lifting of a tea cup, the sound of your name in someone else's mouth, the glance sculpting years of recognition—not one seemed small enough for words. But art— that could begin to hold a life, all the dark curves and jagged edges. Mae ponders again her upcoming show. She thinks of those she's loved these last decades. She does not know how the people she calls her family will react.

She is most concerned about Lauren. After Mae retired from teach-ing, she moved to the other side of this small Ohio town to that one-story brick home where her best friend, Eva, had lived. After Eva died at 60, her daughter, Lauren, offered Mae first choice of renting the house—not even renting, really, just occupying and paying the utilities. It was just two houses from where Lauren and her accountant husband were starting their family. How could Mae say no? She had known Lauren since she was a shy, introspective twelve-year-old intrigued by music. When Lauren and her mother had moved to town, the two had performed family duets on the organ at Mae's church. It was there the young girl came alive, her thin legs stretching to push the pedals, her eyes lost in the vibration of notes.

It was the love of the arts, of worship, and of children that brought Mae and Eva together. Both were women without a husband (Mae never had one; Eva's died in war when Lauren was young) in a church where men were the deacons and ushers. In her mind, when she thought of these men at all, they were standing stiffly at doors and under archways, pointing this way or that. Their suits were the dull gray of granite. They used words like road signs or exhibit titles—short and practical. Their presence was helpful but not substantial.

But the arts—music, painting, even Sunday school crafts and sanctuary "decorations"—these were the sole domain of the women, and Mae and Eva took them on together. They organized church luncheons complete with tea sandwiches, organ recitals, "tasteful" flower arrangements, and invitations with precise calligraphy. After two months of a class they called "Painting by Verses," they led the Sunday school teens in transforming one wall of the Fellowship Hall into a depiction of The Last Supper. The younger children made stained-glass windows out of colored cellophane and earlier—for Palm Sunday—choreographed their own dance of palms, complete with pirouettes and grand jetés. Mae remembers the pre-teen Lauren helping with both: a brush in hand, adjusting the tint of Judas' hair, and with second-grader Jenny Mather, holding her hand as she attempted arabesque.

Most often, though, Mae thinks how she and Eva read Bible passages aloud to each other, then tried to convey their essence through notes or form. Their experiences of awe similar, their expressions of such nonetheless remained different though complementary. Where Mae questioned, Eva encouraged. Where Eva doubted, Mae clarified. "In the beginning was the Word. . . ." Eva had recited one Sunday afternoon in her kitchen, then stepped quickly to the parlor to bring alive the beginning of Copland's "Appalachian Spring."

Mae, on the other hand, had immediately envisioned bold charcoal lines streaked across a canvas as large as a refrigerator. All she had wanted to do was bow down. She had opened her sketchpad and begun the first confident strokes of what later became an abstract rendition of Creation. Near the end, she had positioned her own form in the lower left-hand corner: small, prostrate, alone.

Even so, she had felt less alone with Eva than with anyone else. That they could share the intimacy of prayer—of both doubt and belief—in a small way made up for the expected institution of marriage that Mae had wanted but somehow missed. It was companionship, not romance, that she felt had eluded her. It was the symmetry of family.

Having no children of her own, such proximity to family was at times enough for Mae. Sundays after church, while Mae and Eva sat lazily in Eva's kitchen, sipping tea and talking, Lauren was always nearby drawing pictures or practicing her scales. Her slight movements were the backdrop to their conversations. The shape of her shadow added to their light.

Often, of course, the proportions had shifted. Groupings had naturally realigned themselves. Some Sundays, Mae would paint the mother and daughter playing at Eva's organ together or leaning against the magnolia tree in their backyard, sharing a memory. At these times, it was enough to be the one recording the relationship—the artist observing. It gave her time to step away, to see the forms anew and how they adjusted to each other in different light. And, of course, there were the times when Mae was absent altogether, when she was not even there to observe but across town at her own apartment, in a life she sometimes forgot was separate from this other duo.

Still, she had created with them more than a decade of such mother/ daughter portraits—from twelve-year-old Lauren in braces to the new bride handing her bouquet to a kerchiefed and frail Eva determined to play at her daughter's wedding. In those last months of struggle, Lauren had performed at church alone. Sometimes, though, with her daughter's help, the old Eva had resurfaced, had leaned into her own organ, sounding her notes vehemently, passionately, running over the more polished, careful playing of her daughter. Those days, both Mae and Lauren had applauded.

When, in her will, Eva had left the organ to Mae but the room to Lauren, both were surprised. They knew one couldn't be separated from the other. Eva's music belonged to both of them, but only within the context of the home she had created. When the lawyer added that Eva had left the study to Mae but the deed to Lauren, their surprise transformed into a slow, soothing understanding. For a week, both dwelt in their own quiet grieving. Then, as if Lauren were simply arranging to again pick Mae up for church, the younger woman offered up her mother's home. It was a type of sharing she had grown used to. Lauren's entire family helped Mae move the following month. The girls carried her paints and clay. Daniel helped Lauren with the paintings, pottery, and statues. The moving men he hired did the rest. When the transition was over, the first thing Mae did was hang the mother/daughter portraits facing the organ. Without a word, both women understood each other's gratitude.

Now, a decade after Eva's death, the house sustained, developed, and redefined these connections: the kitchen where Mae and Lauren drank tea together, the parlor where Sunday afternoons Lauren and her girls huddled close at the organ, Eva's decent-sized study that got the morning light and became Mae's studio, and the two-minute walk to a family Mae could claim.

Mae was Me-Ma to Lauren and Daniel's girls: Elizabeth Eve, 11, and Mae Lynn, 9. Last summer, she had again sketched their portraits in the small backyard: Lizzie, her arms crossed in defiance near the rosebushes; Mae Lynn, dreamy-eyed and upside down, dangling by her knees from the magnolia tree. Of course, they had made her promise these portraits would also be in the upcoming show. It was not a promise Mae had thought she could make. Instead, she had nodded that they—each sister separately or together—would certainly be present.

And so she started another portrait of the girls, but for this one there was no sitting—at least not one of which they were aware. She began in secret, moving the organ bench to her studio and covering it whenever Lauren knocked at the back door. The mahogany became a magnolia branch with Mae Lynn's dangling knees. On the young girl's nail-polished toes, Eva's eyes winked. Everywhere magnolia blossoms opened in welcome.

When she was finished, Mae propped the bench up vertically near the keyboard. She brought in more portraits of Eva and Lauren, of Lauren and her girls, of Lauren and Daniel, and of the girls together and individually. Once she talked the newspaper boy into helping her; three times the mailwoman. She covered the parlor walls with the family's faces and bodies. Then she stood back and observed the crowded room. Twice she lost her balance, but started again. She moved "Prayer" to the forefront, just inside the front door. Its hands lifted toward the instrument.

Those days when a concerned Lauren called, Mae feigned a cold. When Lizzie and Mae Lynn wandered over, she blamed exhaustion. When her "inherited" nieces begged to come in, the older woman admitted she was working hard on the "secret" exhibit and that she wanted to wait until she was finished before showing even them. She would visit them soon in their home, she promised.

When she did, they ran to her with *Super Good!* scrawled across the top margins of math tests. Lauren made Mae's favorite meal— Blanquette de Veau—while Daniel explained, again, how to report income on any artwork she would sell. Then Mae announced that she had spoken to the director of the Community Center and that the exhibit could now be at her home. She would, she explained, note the change of location on her calligraphy invitations.

Just afterwards, when she glanced at Lauren, Mae couldn't interpret the canvas of her face. Too quickly, her friend's daughter stood to clear the dishes. Once at the sink, her back turned, Lauren added, "Of course, we'll all help." A second later, Daniel smiled his half-smile, gathered the dirty silverware, then asked, "Mae, how about some dessert to fatten up those bones of yours?" The girls, anticipating a place in the exhibit, jumped up and down, then danced around the room, striking poses and chanting "Me-Ma, Me-Ma." That night, Mae had begun work on the lower-left leg of Eva's organ.

Now, weeks later, Mae stands back from her work on "Self, Diving" and walks into the parlor to study the transformed instrument. Intricately painted seaweed spirals around the dark wood of each leg and up toward the keys. On the back panel, she has outlined Lizzie's foot tapping the rhythm from her iPod. Eva's praying face hovers in the background. On one side panel, Lauren—standing tiptoe on the top of a cross—reaches for a half note that dangles from one of her mother's raised hands. On the opposite panel, Mae has painted in oils her charcoaled rendition of Creation. On the organ's front piece, she has shaped the dead and smiling Eva, huddled together with her daughter and granddaughters beside the magnolia. In the background—and much smaller—Mae has drawn a pregnant replica of herself bringing to life the promised family portrait. Even now, Mae imagines Eva's impromptu performance of "Appalachian Spring." The elderly artist stands back and stares. What is the best way to give the illusion of music? To suggest the notes of someone's life? After all this, she is still not sure.

She walks back to her studio, then turns again to the unfinished statue.

She pinches the fluid blades into more definite waves. She adds note-shaped leaves to the climbing seaweed. Again using her metal teasing needle, she heightens the illusion of tightened calf muscles atop the layered water. What is beyond the statue refuses to be known. Under water, sound waves bend differently. Once she accepts such changes, she will let the clay harden to the leather stage. Then she will need to cut open the figure and hollow it out. Otherwise, it will explode during firing. As she learned long ago, only at 1100 degrees will the necessary transformation take place.

She knows just where she'll position the finished statue: on the top edge of Eva's organ and closest to the side door where her frequent guests will exit. She may need to change the work's title. She may need, at 75, to learn how to swim. It should not be that difficult to teach herself.

Woman's First Skydive Turns Out to Be Her Last

Williamsport Sun-Gazette headline

August 15, 2005

X.

RIPCORD: THE FINE LINE between thrill and terror. Fear billows breath into wind. That Saturday, witnesses gave conflicting reports. Tandem with her instructor, Julia jumped. On that they all agreed. They cheered the two distant bodies in flight, watched as the air cooperated. What they disagreed on was the building at the north end of Ogden Airport. When the sudden gust pushed, were the concrete blocks right there? Did the bodies first hit cinder? Or, as others insisted, did the parachute simply collapse? In the guise of wind, the unexpected can squeeze out the cloth's air, drop divers instantly to asphalt.

IX.

"Particularly tragic," explained Fire Department Battalion chief Steven Splinter. "Many of the witnesses were family. What could be said? They saw it all."

VIII.

I had told my sister not to try. What is the point of risk? A false sense of strength? The lie that you're invincible? Look at the instructor: ten years of training. Trust, I told her, has nothing to do with it. Damn it, it's an airplane. I don't care who's jumping with you.

VII.

I admit it. Every time he took someone new, I was jealous. It was how we'd met—the long hours of instruction, the careful preparation, and finally the plunge into that vast blank of air. Exhilarating, yes. How can I explain it to anyone else? He was young and had just started teaching. I held his hand and jumped. All alone together in the clouds. The earth coming up toward us. The two of us. The world.

    Was it the same with the others?

VI.

Unlike my other children, Julia couldn't wait to be born. From the first, everything about her was emergency. I was grocery shopping when the cramps hit and doubled me over. Next thing I knew, I was on the floor by a stack of canned baked beans, Jessica, Joannie, and Jo all crying. Someone must have called the ambulance, packed up the kids, and contacted my husband. How? I don't know. All I remember were sirens, the rush of doctors, and going under into that sea of forgetfulness. Of course, they slashed my belly and got her out, my impatient one. Her heart almost stopped beating; she was blue from the get-go. That was my Julia. Always on her way to someplace else. Scaring us. Wishing we had her gumption.

V.

She was my youngest but most impulsive daughter. At three, she wanted to be a fighter pilot like my own dad. At six, she climbed up on the roof to help me paint. Scared my wife to pieces, but she was OK up there. So confident and sure of her footing. Some Saturdays, I'd take her over to the local airport, just Julia, and we'd count the airplanes, talk about both of our dreams. It was one of those father/daughter things you hear folks talk about but don't understand until it's you. Same with this.

IV.

It was all by the book. Routine. I'd worked with Vancleave before, had flown hundreds of drops. I assure you, nothing like this had ever happened. I can tell you this, though, she was happy. Ecstatic, really. Wouldn't stop talking about reaching her dream, making it. There was going to be a party afterwards. A real shindig. Right before she dove, she invited me.

III.

I was checking flights on the computer when I saw them in my peripheral vision. At least I think I did. What I thought was, "There I am, finally doing what I want. Unafraid." You know how sometimes you see yourself in others. Eerie. It must have been the split second before. I turned back to my computer. Then the sirens. The sirens.

II.

The instructor, Vancleave, is out of the hospital. The parachutes are checked, double-checked, and packed; the plane all gassed up. Here we are on the runway. Don't just sit there.

I.

Begin.

Weeds

THE SUMMER I WAS nine, Laura-Lynn Boglio and I made a chain of dandelions that stretched around our small brick house. "If the chain breaks," she warned, "someone in your house will die." (We never stretched the weeds around her house next door. Her father was already ill.) In the evenings, she sat on my back porch, sipping black cows and flicking the yellow tops in my face. "Your Mama had a baby and its head popped off," we'd scream, then rub the "butter" of the weeds on each other's necks. Such pronouncements were as much a part of our lives as not stepping on sidewalk cracks.

I never knew how these rituals got started. Perhaps it was a childish instinct to protect and confirm that protection. Maybe we wanted the option of revenge. Did we really "accidentally" miss the square or "inadvertently" tug the chain too hard? Did we do it on purpose? It was as mixed up in our heads as the beauty of the dandelions that threatened to destroy our front lawns.

Laura-Lynn and I had decided long before that we were soul sisters who had gotten split into two different households. And because we were the only only-children on a street where most homes had five or six non-adults to hug and kiss or pinch and kick, we knew that we were somehow marked in a way that the others weren't. We hoped we were singled out, not left out. There was something about being chosen, especially on June nights when you had picked clean half a dozen dandelions to make yellow blush, that left you knowing that what you said or did on the outside was completely unimportant—or that these, in fact, were the only essentials of life, the only things that you could hang onto.

What happened to Laura-Lynn and me all that summer, though most of the time seemed not so out of the ordinary, was perhaps the beginning of everything we both fear and love and why the two mix so perfectly in the childhood of our adult lives. Even now we cannot whisper about it across telephone lines that pretend to stretch around our houses and tug us closer, threatening at any moment to snap, to break. There are no more small brick houses, and even if we could see far enough across two states, I'm not sure we would recognize each other (except for the spot on the chin where the yellow should be) where we were chosen, where we were marked by what on the surface looks beautiful but destroys.

Jimmy, Laura-Lynn's eighteen-year-old cousin from three towns over, came often enough the first part of that summer and then often and then not at all. He was a gangly kid with hair that wouldn't stay down no matter how often you spit on it and a nose that ended a little sooner than you expected. On evenings when he stretched out on our back porch full of root beer and ice cream, he didn't burp but hiccupped with the rhythm of respirators. His legs were a full yard longer than ours, but his torso was shrunk as if it had forgotten to grow at the same speed, so that he was not quite as tall as would have been expected. What we didn't know was why he sat with us all sprawled out, him being older and a boy, and us only relatives or nearly. Nor could we grasp why he thought he was a doctor, because he did—not in the sense that it had already happened because anyone knew that, but in the sense that it was already decided. To him, it seemed a matter only of time and money, the latter of which Laura-Lynn and I doubted he would ever get working at diners and bowling alleys or, as a last resort, for small change caring for a dying uncle.

Still he practiced diagnosis like a ritual, telling us how our ice cream slid down our throats and what churned and curled it from there. On the days he stayed, he sat hours in the family room next to Mr. Boglio, listening, he told us, for the opening and closing of valves and the fluttering of lungs. He could tell, even in his sleep, if his uncle rolled more heavily than before or if his breathing came a little too staccato, things which Laura-Lynn's mother had long since forgotten and became more and more distanced to in her own room.

At the time it all seemed not so different from my own parents who smiled but rarely touched. In both houses there was the sense that something would or would not happen, growing as secretly as tumors you never find. This is not to say that we labeled ourselves as sad or happy, or that we knew what we felt at all—except in brief moments where there was no yellow sun and no night, those few moments before sleep when we knew the little over which we had control.

But Jimmy, we thought, knew at least where to look for it, pouring over a library copy of *Gray's Anatomy* in his cutoffs, sucking on the end of a dandelion, and smirking as if even on this block, in these houses, life was too obvious.

Laura-Lynn's hair was not as brown as Jimmy's, but she had the same habit of pushing back the short bangs when she thought. Some afternoons, like twins, they would push at their bangs in rhythm, chanting different parts of the brain. For every name they missed, they claimed that they lost a brain cell. It seemed, then, smarter to me not to play at all and risk no loss, but to do so would also mean losing a place in the huddle of three—something I could not afford. We'd then hold hands and circle, a more grown-up version of "Ring Around the Rosy" with dandelions for substitutes. When I held both Jimmy's and Laura-Lynn's hand—his rough with knotty fingers, hers tiny but always with one or two Band-Aids like tourniquets on the fingers—I knew that both words and thoughts passed from hand to hand, up through the arms, and out our mouths. And so I held both as tightly as I could, trying to make us a family. Were we? "Gyrus rectus, island of Reil, fissure of Sylvius," I half-sang until I knew where and why my head hurt and how our chant was an oath of something I had not yet discovered.

Other days we dramatized the action of the heart, huddling together, then loosening, contracting, expanding, and muttering, "pa-pa-pa-pa-pa-pa-pa-pa-pa-pa-pa," as we tilted around the backyard, faster and faster until, out of breath and out of control, we fell, laughing on the solid ground.

These afternoons, however, were not as common as those which Jimmy spent inside with the uncle he barely knew, reading aloud Ecclesiastes or passing the bed pan while his aunt, in a cramped rented office across town, typed insurance policies for the not-yet-dying. I tried to stay as much out of the room as possible and as far away from the word "cancer" as I could. There were times, though, that I remember leaning on the half-opened door—waiting for Laura-Lynn to find a bicycle pump, a cup for a bundle of wildflowers, or her father's new medicine—when I saw Jimmy as a different boy, his gray eyes steady on his sleeping uncle, the hint of shadow in his eyes.

At these times, he never acknowledged seeing me, and I, even at nine, knew he was right; we were both too young to know much of what was beyond the closed lids. I was afraid to know too much of anything about adults. Life in my own house was decided every two weeks when my father was home from his route, and my mother never bothered me with her doubts, though in retrospect, life must certainly have frightened her. Her face had that kind but guarded look as if one escaped secret on her part would cause an avalanche of worry too big for even my father's truck to haul away. And I was to be protected.

Jimmy, too, I thought, wanted to protect, and that was why he did not look at me as I clung to the doorknob. And I, too, wanted to protect my near-brother Jimmy and Laura-Lynn, my mother and father, and anyone else who thought it was actually possible to be strong. And so I always looked past Jimmy at these times to Laura-Lynn's father who, in fact, understood what wasn't possible to protect and so didn't even try.

That was why Laura-Lynn and I started the second dandelion chain, the one, if it had to, could go around both of our houses, maybe even around our entire block—although we didn't want to increase the chance of breakage or its power by including too many of the abundant weeds. We worked furiously when Jimmy wasn't with us, tugging the near translucent stalks clean at their base, then twisting and tying tail to head, the way we had once laid, foot to head, grabbing each other's ankles to imitate a giant spinal cord. Some dandelions had already closed themselves off to the world, a seemingly innocuous Venus flytrap, a turtleneck of green pressing in the gold. Others were hairballs ready to float. Some were only gangly bodies, abandoned. Meticulously, we tied. A few of the older ones soon lost their shaggy manes and grayed, and we had to replace them. But most defied expiration and hung, somewhat limply, one after the other, in a long chain along the side of the house.

When Jimmy sprawled out on the grass near us (we weren't allowed to bring them on the back porch), he never helped. Instead, he talked incessantly about the length of large intestines or the yards of skin donated each year for operations. Every once in a while, though, I saw him tuck a dandelion in his pocket or tug at the yellow strands with his teeth. Sometimes we broke down and painted each other's faces. These times, he'd join in, pressing a lightning rod Indian-style across my forehead or down the front of Laura-Lynn's neck, just inches above her small breasts. I'd hold my breath and wait for his hand to slip, but all through July, he never batted an eye. Laura-Lynn kept laughing.

On the days Jimmy helped take his uncle to the hospital, and later when the nurse would come on Tuesdays and Thursdays, I had to work on the chain by myself, watching, as the car pulled away, Laura-Lynn's stiffly set jaw, her mother's vacant eyes, and Jimmy's square but sloping shoulders behind the wheel. On those days, I added an extra knot to each of the linked weeds.

We never finished that second chain. We had gotten enough to make it three-quarters around my house with only snapping the rope two or three times while trying to measure it. Laura-Lynn and I had been working on it several hours one August morning when the sun beat down so fiercely on our backs, we were sure its dandelion face was tattooed on our reddening shoulders. Both our mothers were working that day, and we were out of root beer and ice cream. We hooked up the hose, scrambled into our bathing suits (both yellow with black polka dots), and laughed our way in and out of the spray. The grass was long (I was supposed to cut it two days before) and scratched at our feet, a pleasant irritation. We were only missing Jimmy, but after about ten minutes, he peeked his head out the screen door and pranced out in his cutoffs, yelping hilariously up and down the backyard as we took turns jabbing him with the hard water.

All dripping wet, we painted our stomachs with yellow smiley faces, using the part of the chain that had gotten caught in the crossfire and thus hung limper than ever. Then Jimmy traced our spinal chords, reciting, "cervical, dorsal, lumbar, sacrum, coccyx," carefully describing the ways the vertebrae shattered when a guy in his high school dove off a cliff toward water that was too shallow. We didn't want to hear another tragedy. We didn't want to know, and so Laura-Lynn and I, with Jimmy pretending to chase us, ran around and around my house. On the sixth time around, I ducked in our back door, hoping to trick the others but also to grab my favorite T-shirt before they caught on. Unable at first to find it, I trotted wet footprints through all four rooms before tugging the T-shirt from beside the toilet and tub.

When I got back outside, Laura-Lynn and Jimmy were gone, the hose had stopped dripping, and there was a wonderful sense of secrecy in the mid-afternoon air. I snuck toward Laura-Lynn's side door and opened it a crack, the click the faint sound of wet fingers snapping. As usual, her father was in the family room, his hospital bed propped up and facing the kitchen. He turned his face slightly. His eyes, dark and haunting, were the most awake I'd ever seen them. He stared at me a full three seconds. The kitchen light reflected on their surface as if a lone candle were flickering in the room. There was something in them I had never seen, and I stood still, knowing that I had somehow trespassed into his other world, that perhaps he had already died and was glaring at me from the other side, or perhaps wanted to take me there with him. He looked at me as if we would never be separated. I wanted to smile or cry or nod, but I didn't move. I couldn't. Three long seconds and then he closed his eyes.

It was then that I saw what he had seen, what he was watching when I had carefully unlatched the door and even now as I stood there with it cracked a few inches. Jimmy was in the kitchen, directly behind Laura-Lynn and against her, washing the yellow from her stomach with a ragged dishcloth and soap. No one was giggling. His one hand held her wrist tightly. Her arm was red and tensed. Jimmy's other hand began at her belly button and moved in circles outward, again and again, now cleaning flesh that was only flesh-colored and already clean. When he reached the hem of her bikini top, he pushed the cloth upward and in, continuing to circle until the material loosened enough for one small nipple, the center of a new flower, to show between his fingers. His wrist still under the suit, he continued pushing upward, soaping her throat until every trace of yellow disappeared and suds dripped under her partially raised top. Laura-Lynn was vacantly staring at the sink, away from me and away from her father, who now kept his eyes closed, the way we were used to seeing him and always assumed he would be as we giggled and told each other secrets over lemonade. (Which of our private thoughts had he heard? And what else did he know about his daughter?) Jimmy continued wiping my best friend's skin with a clean dishcloth and new water, moving in and out of the yellow and black bottoms and top until every trace of soap was gone and Laura-Lynn stood, teeth starting to chatter, in a small puddle.

And then I crashed open the door and yelled, "ice cream," me with the yellow streaks still on my stomach, a seal that had not been broken. At that moment, Jimmy let the dishcloth flop on the counter, the way he always did when helping with the dishes. Laura-Lynn nervously washed her hands at the sink and mopped up the floor. Her father kept his eyes closed and his breathing steady. I knew that he was awake, that he had seen the beginning of what I didn't want to know, had perhaps seen it often, and that he would, like I would now also do for years and years, close my eyes, one of us as weak and helpless as the other.

Laura-Lynn grabbed a terrycloth cover-up and, with me, headed out the door toward the ice cream truck we knew would come in the next few minutes, every day at the same time. Jimmy nodded toward his uncle, put his finger to his lips to quiet us, and took a seat next to the hospital bed.

We were both three blocks away before Laura-Lynn and I realized that neither of us had even a cent. We didn't say a word and walked right on past the clanging truck, the sidewalks crowded with big sisters and little brothers, and big brothers and little sisters, tugging at each other's hands or fighting over a few shiny quarters and dimes. We kept going until we reached the school playground, unusually empty, where we swung in silence high and higher for over an hour, but never upside down so our swimsuits showed.

When we got back to Laura-Lynn's, her mother had just come in from work and was fixing herself half a tuna fish sandwich. As usual, she looked tired, ringlets of brown curling around the nape of her neck and sweat beading up on her forehead. Laura-Lynn's father was vacantly staring at a rerun of *Jeopardy!* and Jimmy was doing a crossword on medical terms. As for my mother, she wouldn't be home for another two or so hours.

And so we didn't say a word—to each other or anyone there. Laura-Lynn's father never again looked at me, but I often watched him from the corner of my eye as he slipped in and out of what I thought must be this world and the next. His eyes glazed, his mouth sagged, but he did not die, cradling in his almost-empty body a secret I could not tell my best friend— my near sister—because she had not yet told me. In fact, Laura-Lynn's father lived long after Jimmy left that next week to counsel at camp and a year after the family moved to the next town where the insurance from Mrs. Boglio's new job could pay for better care.

But beginning on that day until Laura-Lynn moved, I mowed, neatly and evenly, both of our lawns, grateful, each moment in the hot sun, for every chopped yellow head that floated on the green before the lawnmower chewed up any trace of the ugly weed.

Nonsmoking Section

PERHAPS SOMEONE HAD THROWN them out a car window. Someone else had flattened them with their tires—there, smack in the middle of the road, residential area. "Whatever," as her best friend from Roosevelt Middle School, Anita, liked to say. Now the smashed cellophane package of cheap cigars was hidden under a game of Clue in her closet. She wouldn't even tell Anita, much less her parents.

The first night she watched until her digital clock clicked to 2:25, then reached for her flashlight and headed for the closet. She found the package quickly, half the length of her notebook ruler, only as wide as an Oreo. There were two cigars, smashed enough that brown curlicues, like pencil shavings, clung to the ends. She tilted the package side to side until they slide, dun confetti, first to one end, then the other. She raised the contraband to her nose and inhaled.

The next night, she awoke at 12:46 and made her way without the flashlight. She had been dreaming of tall towers of flames. Of airplanes. When she raised the tobacco to her teeth, the cellophane broke freely, a pungent smell of stale reaching her nostrils.

She slept with the cigars beneath her pillow. Of course, she had seen the cigarette movies, how smoke clouded the inside of your lungs, leaving large, deadly spots. Of course, she had heard her uncles hacking, had gone to their funerals with her parents. But these were the cigars of young millionaires considering financial deals, of old men in velvet smoking jackets, of Professor Plum deducing who killed whom with what in the library.

After a week, she took a deep breath and chose one, surprised at how naturally the V of her fingers held its shape, such slight pressure needed to keep it steady. She tried the second cigar with her other hand. Though they looked the same, even in her inexperience, she could feel the difference of texture. She wondered about lighting the tips, taking in the smoke—the seemingly careless control. She practiced. She practiced.

Eiffel Tower

WHAT I REMEMBER MOST is him asking about it in the middle of making love, how it was, the Eiffel Tower, I mean, when I went up there with someone else. It was not romantic, the question, I mean, AND the Tower, truth tangled up in words. I contemplated looking believable, which I was. I pondered speaking slowly, which I did. But he had already made up my memory.

Once, walking arm in arm through an art museum gift store, we saw a six-inch glass replica of the landmark. After he smashed it, a cashier with a Renoir pin of Women Bathing politely asked him to leave. It was $5.99. She said nothing to me.

The action of the wind on the tower is reduced by the hydraulic caissons into which the feet are firmly fixed.

An innocent can only count former kisses by seconds, which I did. The difference between five and six seconds was a slap and a hit. I was always honest, hellfire a threat that loomed in my Sunday school mind, still sweet sixteen though twenty-three. "She who looks upon a man has already committed…." Anticipating rage, I threw away prom pictures, inscribed books, cheap heart-shaped jewelry. I couldn't throw away the Eiffel Tower, its proud beams jutting up where I least expected them: on calendars, wall clocks, movie posters, breakfast cereal boxes, the King's Island amusement park. That first summer, I burned five tour books and a diary.

It took Eiffel two years to build his steel construction. The tower has three floors: the first at 57 m, the second at 115 m, the third at 276 m. It was a television transmitter for the greater Paris region.

Do you hear what I'm saying? Am I transmitting anything? It took 1,829 days to ask all his questions. It took 7,342 to stop answering. If I look closely, I can see me from here. It's twenty years ago. I'm waving from the top floor. I'd never heard of phallic symbols. Wish you were there.

On a fine day, the view from the top platform is over the whole of Paris and even the more distant suburbs. You can't imagine Paris without it.

The imagination is always better or worse than the actual event. The slope of the steel. The Seine below. The distant sounds of made-up memories. He couldn't imagine what he'd started, that acquaintance from school, watching the same famous view. Shy. Too afraid to brush my hand. Not saying a word, much less in French. *Je ne sais rien.* Are you surprised by such naiveté? Admit it. Even you, a stranger, are a little jealous of a new groom's imagination. Sometimes I am.

The 12,000 steel girders are held together by 2,500,000 rivets to produce a smooth, curving profile. Its functional elegance heralded the dawn of Industrial Art, and has met with much sarcastic comment from more conservative observers since it was finished in 1889.

Tell me, how many seconds did you kiss? What color were the city lights? What did you tell the others who came later? I won't breathe a word, I promise, not even under duress.

Permanent

BEFORE THE PARAMEDICS ARRIVE, the father tucks in his four-year-old daughter and surrounds her with twenty-two stuffed animals and assorted photographs. In five, she is sitting in his lap. In eight, she is at an amusement park. In two more, she is hugging a stuffed lamb. In one, she is eating Rice Krispies. Her head is carefully propped on the bed's ruffled pillow. Later, the police count a dozen stab wounds. If Shout were applied immediately to the sheets, the stains would dissolve into temporary.

At the playground, the week before, she played with my son on the short slide, both too afraid of heights. Her father waved when she reached the top. My son gave a thumb's up, his victory temporary when he slipped and fell. There was no permanent damage.

At home, we cleaned the un-bleeding knee, adhered Spiderman bandages. My son asked about the little girl, if she'd made it down OK. I had forgotten to look but answered immediately. He did not question my truthfulness.

In the future, when my daughter trips and breaks her nose, we ignore the speed limit getting her to the hospital. My son worries about the police, watches out the window for their flashing disk, insists he can hear a siren. Inside the emergency room, the nurses look at me suspiciously. They ask me again how it happened. Before this conversation takes place, I will need to rehearse a scenario.

Today, I wait impatiently in the waiting room, reading Power Ranger books to my son. When he falls asleep, I scan the local paper, looking for the trial, and how long the father will be in. After an hour, the nurse asks me why I'm there. "No reason," I say, trying to sound temporary.

Memory often re-arranges events, adds elaborate details. More often than not, the effect is permanent. You will forget this detail immediately after it is read.

Lot's Daughters

Genesis Ch. 19

I.

AT FIRST—A LEERING MOB circling the house, jeering, dancing naked, taunting the guests with their sex—the daughters thought their father brave to step outside, lock the door behind him, stretch his arms out in protection. But then, even he offered them up, a sacrifice to protect strangers. Their father, the only "righteous man" in a city destined for flames, "Do with them what you like. But don't do anything to these men." Then their eyes were like Isaac's below the knife, the ram not yet in the bush, the blade gleaming.

II.

What dread dug in the daughters' betrayed hearts before the rioters—struck blind—stumbled and fell, unable to find the door, Lot tugged back safely to the house? Eyes straight toward Zoar, did they hear their mother turning, nostalgia sliced mid-sentence? That life left behind, what fixed their gaze away from home—their father's almost-sacrifice or the intervention?

III.

No mention of mourning. Their mother's unbelief behind them. Too many miles. The sun hot as horror.

IV.

When they fled to the cave with no hope for heirs, ashen cities behind them, mercy was an unremembered flame. This time, they sacrificed themselves, holding out wine, lifting their dresses to lure their father. He twirled himself a drunken dance, love or revenge spinning, blurring vision. "Rewarded" with sons, they named them *From Father* and *Son of My People*, then sang lullabies of fear and fire, of what it means to wander, to exile yourself, to dream of salt and sand.

Rough Drafts

I DIDN'T PLAN THIS type of life. I'm always punctual; I always do things well. But Monday my second week at the job, I'm still scurrying around the bathroom at 8:56 a.m.—a quick rinse with Scope, a swipe with the blush—when I jab myself right in the eye with mascara. My eyes start tearing; the brown-black mascara is everywhere.

I splash my eyes with water and then dab at the black with toilet paper. The mascara's about gone—just a smear under my right eye. The mirror, still streaked from last month's tenants, smudges bits of my face in the reflection, my chin and left eyebrow both blurry. I look more tired than usual; my face, thinner, longer. Behind me in the mirror, hose hang off the shower rod; last week's newspaper sits on the back of the john. "What a dump," I think, but it's exactly what I want: two rooms in an old house, a town of unfamiliar faces.

I'm about to finish the job with cotton swabs. My eyes are deep set and shadows catch below them, but I see mascara in the curve and the slight indent below the eye. I slow and touch the spot with a finger. This seems important: the dim light in the bathroom, the way I can't hear if I'm breathing, not as if I'm alone, but as if I'm not here at all. Slowly, I blend the mascara into skin to make a soft grey and then dab foundation over the top. If my right eye matched the left, it'd look like lack of sleep. It's that subtle. I practice looking down, looking suspicious, looking nowhere.

I think of carefully folding tissue into my bra at age thirteen. I held my breath for ten seconds before tiptoeing down the stairs into the kitchen and giving the cold shoulder to Mom's oatmeal, to her quick-clipped talk, to the way she sipped her coffee as if inhaling the only good in the world. I avoided her eyes and let the screen door clack shut as loudly as possible. I slouched like a spy the whole twelve blocks to school, but once there I loved being ordinary. Back arched, chest out, I strutted past lockers and the secrets they held, glad to be like everyone I'd ever known: average. Only Carla Ortella noticed the slight rounding of my breasts.

I think of spending babysitting money on turtleneck after turtleneck. Every color imaginable: pink, chartreuse, fuchsia, and berry red—colors to hide the marks of pretended passion, colors to hide that there was nothing to hide. Some weeks I'd pinched my neck before tugging on a sweater, just to know something was there, something that shouldn't show.

And I think of winter: standing on the porch in a snowstorm and eating an apple, biting right into the bruise, hearing no crunch. The bruise of that apple. The shadow below my eye. I wash my hands and try to forget, to think of nothing. But when I head downstairs and walk around the corner, the bus is pulling away.

It's 9:40 by the time I slip into the office. The copyeditors are staring at their desks, pretending to think in complete sentences, carefully punctuating everyone else's dreams. They sit poised, ready to delete paragraphs and restructure thoughts.

This wasn't a job I wanted, but it's as good a place as any. It isn't where I was before. Here I can delete things that aren't important, things that aren't rugs under someone's feet. Here a question mark has never seen *How will I live?* or *Where will I go?* And *therefore* is only a word, a transition without plans.

I think of the way children cry when you're leaving, in gasps, trying to breathe in the last of you. Then I think how much it can hurt to breathe, the weight on your chest, and how all of this has nothing to do with now or here or with people I barely know within arm's reach day after day.

* * *

By the time I settle in for my second week, the editorial staff is well into the third chapter of a 300-page book tentatively entitled *The Great Fake Out: Religion in the Public Arena.* On the bulletin board above my desk, my coworker, Luanne, has thumbtacked APRIL 21, the book's deadline. It's February.

Not until after I get coffee and pull my chair close to the desk does she nod and look at her watch. She blinks her eyes slowly, brushes hair from her forehead, and then winks and hands me a doughnut. "A worm for the early bird," she says. I think maybe this is supposed to be a joke, but now she's frowning. I can tell she hates me—that they all hate me. No doubt they finished their coffee and were reading copy by 9:05, all in a row like this, looking meticulous, stereotypically neat, and efficient. They look at me like I've really screwed up, as if my absence has caused the deletion of whole chapters, as if the first page of the book will now read "Chapter 3: Recognizing Wolves," and an errata will be glued, book by book, to the back page: "Due to an illness beyond one copyeditor's control, Chapters 1-2 have been omitted."

In a passage describing co-hosts on Bible talk shows, I change *She ruins her life* to *He or she ruins his or her life*—more awkward yet more accurate. I remove *you must surrender.* Wherever *submission* appears, I cross it out and write *repression.* I'm starting to get into this: add something here, take something else away.

But by 11 a.m., I'm getting restless and a bit ticked off that no one's noticed my handiwork. I turn to Luanne, "You think this should be a semicolon or a period?" Then I start to read: "Actually, it's easy to tell the difference between the two; for example, the charlatan—"

"A period," Luanne interrupts. She looks at me, at the page, then at me again, touches her own eye, and incorporates the gesture into brushing back her bangs. "Or a semicolon," she apologizes. What she means is this: *It's not worth fighting over. It doesn't matter.*

* * *

Tuesday I get up by 6:30 and apply my makeup slowly, this time a little darker. I brush brown and pink eye shadow onto my lids and apply eyeliner with a steady hand. I trace my lips with a dark plum gloss and then smack them loudly. The dress I wear is the color of rain.

I get to the office early, sip my coffee black, and spend a half an hour humming to myself and concocting excuses: *I ran into the corner of the cupboard door* or *The ten-year-old brat next door was shooting rubber bands again—just missed my eye.* I don't mention fists or belts or broken plates, but I think them, think them so loudly they fill my head, shatter all over my face. When the others start trickling in, first the receptionist, then Luanne, then the guys in shipping, then my boss, Doug, I sigh dramatically, "So much quieter," as if I've just escaped from a KISS concert. Nobody nods, but they notice me. They know that I live alone, that I just moved here, and that I have no friends—I don't need any.

The guys in shipping cluster around me. They are all six foot or taller and wear Extra Large. There's no way out. They shake my hand in jerks, bark, "Dave, Paul, Vern, Deano, Dan" and demand that I remember, not mix them up. I keep my hand as limp as possible, smile only slightly, and stutter my name. They look me up and down three times, and then ask me if I made the coffee; they tell me it's bitter.

On the way to our separate offices, Doug, a big man with a wide tie, follows me. By my door he's suddenly awkward. "Doing a good job," he stammers. "Coming right along."

I look away. "Yeah, it's coming OK," I say without any conviction whatsoever. Then I leave him standing in the hallway, just where I want him. He doesn't know where to look or what to do.

Later, when Luanne surprises me and asks if I want to go to lunch, I surprise her back. "I'm meeting someone," I say. I don't even look up. But I spend the thirty minutes of lunch alone at the drugstore makeup counter. Cosmetic companies don't know anything; all of their names are stupid: *blushing beige, ravenous red, passionate pink*. What about *abuse-me apricot*? *Spit-at-me-with-your-stale-breath salmon*? Won't fit on the labels? Too much for the average housewife? I take a felt-tipped pen from my purse and think of drawing lines straight as arrows through the adjectives *provocative, tempestuous*, and *sexy*, leaving the colors not strong but by themselves: *peach, turquoise, silver*. Instead, I line the air and then trace the lifeline on my palm.

When I check the price of some foundation, the ink smears on my hand like a cut and comes off on the bottle. I move to the register and hand the clerk $46.30 for burnt-orange blush, tawdry-tan foundation, and three shades of lipstick, all dark. The girl, a teenager, looks me right in the eyes. She knows.

The rest of the week, I decide to dress up, wear my makeup heavy, and consistently arrive fifteen minutes late. I stop at shipping on the way in, steal stamps and scissors, and tie string around my middle finger. I ask for zip codes to Xenia, Fort Knox, and Three Mile Island or the postal rates to Hiroshima and Dachau. When one of the shipping guys looks at me to see if I'm kidding, I stumble over a box and then lean on his arm.

I make sure I'm the last one to finish my coffee. I make sure everyone can tell that I'm nervous and shaky. And then I drop my cup in the hallway. I pretend to try not to cry, and instead I whimper, softly as if under blankets or pillows, as if I can barely breathe. I'm in the corridor by the coffee machine; the others are at their desks. They poke their heads outside their doors and ask, "Have you seen Doug?" or "Have you seen the cover artwork?" or "Does a colon go in or outside of quotation marks?" I answer, "no," "no," and "outside," dabbing coffee off of my blue suit, the one that hangs too loosely on my frame, looser now than ever. I act as if picking up broken pieces of mug is the most natural thing, as if I've done it every morning of my life, as if I'm glad the mug didn't hit me in the head.

I pretend to be embarrassed and look down, and then I suck the blood from a cut on my finger. The piece of mug in my other hand says "THEN YOU DIE." I throw it away with a loud clunk and go back to my desk. Ten minutes later, I realize I've spotted the copy with blood, and I try, unsuccessfully at first, to cover the splotches with Wite-Out.

Everything's going OK when I come to the passage "let not your adornment be merely external, braiding the hair, wearing gold jewelry. . . ." I draw a thin line through the letters. In the margin, I write *Ye shall know a book by its cover; act accordingly*. After the phrase "let it be the hidden person of the heart, with the imperishable quality of a gentle and quiet spirit," I insert *and the mentality of a doormat*. I think of writing Chinese fortunes for a living, crediting stray thoughts to a mystic. I imagine poking pieces of paper between the crisp folds of a cookie. I imagine writing *A stranger will change your life* and having someone—a young man, a girl, or an old lady—wait not in terror but in hope, wait patiently with faith. I partly retract what I've done, writing *STET* next to my changes. Later, when Luanne goes over the page, she erases the markings, corrects the spelling errors I missed (*insubstantel, inigma, renagade*), and doesn't say a word.

I try to work for an hour or so, but things are too quiet, so I put my head in my hands. When Luanne asks if I'm OK, I say "No" and head for the bathroom. In the stall, I stare at the freshly painted door. I touch it with my fingers, then my palm. I take a nickel from my pocket and scratch out a sentence. It's several minutes before I can remember my new phone number, remember which one it is. When I do, I carve the numbers an inch high, watching as the paint chips float, tiny as snow, to the tile. I think of sneaking into the men's restroom and scratching my address, my social security number, and my measurements into the wall beside the urinal. Instead, I clog the toilet with paper towels and watch as it overflows. I move to the fluorescent-lit mirror, reapply my lipstick, and accidentally bite my lip. Blood dries on my chin in a thin line. I don't wash it off.

From then on, someone asks me to lunch everyday. They ask about work, sports, and the weather. I answer as cryptically as I can, "Yes, there were six kids in my family, and we never once fought," or "The fear of the Lord is the beginning of knowledge," or "70% of all married women cheat on their husbands within the first five years." They don't know what to say. They try to laugh, but can't; they try to look sympathetic. Usually they shift uncomfortably in their seats, slurp soup, and say, "Did you see that miracle shot of LeBron's? Just try to stop them now!" or "Heard it's going to hit fifty tomorrow. About time."

* * *

March I start hanging out with the guys in shipping. At work they poke their heads in my office, grin, and ask me how I'm feeling this fine morning. We've got the routine down to a T. After work, we stop at Tony's, buy a couple of rounds, and maybe a few of us wander over to the Wayside. When we walk in, they steer me toward the bar. I learn everyone's drink and how to carry four pitchers of beer at once. On good days, I can dance like this between tables. I can sing. I make up lyrics and pretend they're old. I add my name to the songs, the names of the guys. Some nights I call everyone Joe.

The second week, I start surprising them: cream them in darts, slaughter them in pool. For fun, they try to make me nervous and wolf-whistle every time I lean over for a shot. One asks me my favorite color of ball. Another says to knock 'em hard. As soon as my arm is cocked, someone bumps against me, pretending he's drunk. And always they swear at my last ball as it banks and spins toward the corner. We play snooker, cutthroat, and nine-ball for hours; eight out of ten games I win. All the while, the guys are smiling, waiting. I try to see myself in their eyes, but they move too quickly and won't stand still.

Some nights I look up to see I'm dancing with the wrong man, someone I don't know and haven't met. He knows everything about me: my birthday, my mother's maiden name, and what I like most for breakfast. Sometimes across the bar, I see a woman nodding. She touches her lip, then her eyes, and incorporates the gesture into brushing back her bangs. She nods again, doesn't smile.

* * *

Most nights, I stay out till five o'clock and come into work late with shadows under my eyes. Instead of getting angry, Doug becomes friendlier and more relaxed. He touches my arm in passing and gives me rides home in his new Ferrari. He slips opera tickets in with my paycheck and tells me to take a friend. Some days he calls me into his office, locks the door, and refuses to take any calls. It's then that he asks me about the others, about job morale—do they like him? Are they happy? What do they do for fun? How much do they drink? I play dumb and smile, and then I wink the way the guys in shipping taught me. I start to call him Douglas, holding out the second syllable for two seconds and smiling when I say it. He tells me about his cousin, a stripper on the South Side who changed her name to Lola when she was eighteen. He gives her extra tips to help her out and make her way through college. He tells me a guy in shipping is a voyeur who steals pink lingerie from Sears; the receptionist has had three abortions; Luanne was once a call girl at the Ritz. It's a joke, I think, and I laugh.

On Sunday, Doug wants me to meet him at the track and not tell the others. He's an hour late and swearing. I win $80.70 on an exacta. But his horse loses, so he tears my ticket in half. I try to piece it together with clear fingernail polish, but it doesn't hold. Still, when Doug asks me to his apartment to watch ball, I go and hope that his team will win. He throws potato chips like confetti in the air, slaps me on the back, and screams louder than anyone I know. I cheer with him, though I don't care who wins.

The next week when editing finishes half the book, it gets its own electric pencil sharpener "for a job well done." I get tickets to a charity ball and a $100 bonus. For nothing, absolutely nothing.

I buy myself a silk short-sleeved blouse, ash gray, and wear it to work the next day. "A present," I lie just to make the others self-conscious and eye me over a bit more than usual, "from some man I met last week at the Purple Sunset. I'm talking to him, right, for about ten minutes—big guy with a great tan and muscles like a construction worker, only he claims he's a surgeon—and he hands me a package, says, 'Here, this ain't my size, anyway….'" Of course, by this time whoever's listening knows I'm lying my head off, and they laugh nervously. I see them, though, after lunch or just before quitting time, glance shyly at the bruise below my sleeve. (It only shows when I raise my arm.) Other days, I see their eyebrows twitch at the scratch on my neck or the burn on my lower wrist. I shrug, tell them "tennis, cat, iron" before they can ask. Or, to get them off my back, I say the impossible and wink: "Butch dropped in again. I made his coffee too strong, and he socked me." Or "Look, I didn't want to tell Sam about us, but he had this cord around my neck and…." They roll their eyes and groan. I get the reaction I want.

The next Monday, after we've worked together for over a month, Luanne gives me her number and tells me to call her, so we can get together for a movie, hang out, chat, or hit the clubs. Alone in my apartment, I try to dial the number she gave me, but get the crisis hotline. I hang up before they ask me my name. I check the paper, number by number, and try again in a half an hour, and then an hour.

* * *

In April, the whole staff works late on the book. Some Saturdays we come in by 9:00 a.m., wear jeans, and order out for pizza. I roll up my sleeves so they won't get in the sauce and eat six pieces in one sitting. In the hallway by the coffee machine, I teach Doug to do the tango. He grabs my hand too tightly and won't let me lead. Luanne and I do a line dance and kick out our legs. We make up funny rhymes about the book and other people in the office and then chant them as loudly as we can. Our co-workers clap. We bow and bow again. When we settle down, we work quickly and get twice as much done.

Once, when the others are gone, Doug massages my shoulders and leans over the desk. "This passage here, at the bottom," he says brushing against me, "weakens the entire argument, don't you think? Can you make it stronger? More believable?" I look at him to see what he means, and he's laughing. About what? He raises his hand to his eyes, brushes back his bangs: "then this pilot says to the stewardess…." But it's too late; I've missed the transition.

He starts asking me questions that aren't his business: where I've lived, why I wear long sleeves when it's seventy? I start coming in earlier, staying later. I keep a running record of everyone's errors, including my own, and then leave the list on Doug's desk at the end of the week. I make up charts and timetables, redo stylesheets. For hours, I sit at my desk and hear nothing but the scratch of my pencil. I start getting to the office by 7:00 a.m. to make the first pot of coffee. When I spill hot water and scald my hand, there's no one there to see it, to tell.

* * *

In May I wear summer suits and no underwear and keep my makeup light. I sit outside at lunch and try to get a tan. I smile at only certain people and am promoted. By mid-month, I forget the names of all the guys in shipping, but remain civil. When I see them at wrestling matches, I wave. Twice a week, I bring in gourmet coffee and jelly-filled doughnuts. I eat half the doughnuts myself and give the others to Luanne. I tell them I know a secret and, though they ask me again and again, I won't say what it is. On payday, I stay late with Doug, drinking bourbon, breaking every pencil exactly in half, burning old copies of books, and laughing. When he tells me to sock him in the stomach as hard as I can, I do and I know that I've hurt him. I wait for him to hurt me back. I wait.

Front Door/Back Door

8:27 a.m. Tuesday

WHEN SUZANNE ARRIVED FOR her 8:30 hairdresser's appointment, the police were already there—three of them, their cars parked neatly out front by the curb. They were huddled together, whispering, and pointing. Then they went inside. Of course, the hairdresser, Kayra, was beside herself (who wouldn't be?), running her hands through her long straightened hair, weeping beside the large flashing sign: Hair for You. "Who would do this to me?" she groaned and looked at her nails. "Who?" What could Suzanne do but hug her and wait for the cops' instructions?

8:36 a.m. Tuesday

Kayra was inside when the man sped into the alleyway and parked sideways next to the shop. When he ran up the steps through the front door, Suzanne yelled after him, "Do you know her?" He didn't answer, but once inside, he gave Kayra a long hug and held her hand as they both spoke with the police. Suzanne, who had stayed outside from politeness, saw everything through the large storefront window. She had forgotten her sweater and began to shiver in the crisp morning air.

8:43 a.m. Tuesday

It seemed impolite to leave without saying anything, so Suzanne walked up the front steps, turned the doorknob, and pushed. She was surprised by Kayra's sudden turn, her gasp, her "No, no, wait, Sweetie, don't touch; fingerprints…." But Suzanne was already in the black-and-white tiled waiting room. She was almost to the mauve chair with the hairdryer. The oldest policeman shook his head as Suzanne backed away, past the still-neat stack of *People* magazines and *Inquirers.* "I'll call you, Honey, to reschedule," Kayra said as the front door snapped back into place. But she didn't.

10:21 a.m. Tuesday

After shopping for groceries and dropping off library books for the kids, Suzanne drove the long way home past the hairdresser's. The police cruisers were gone, but the man's slightly rusted Thunderbird was still crooked, there to the alley side of the front door where Suzanne had entered, where she had touched the cold metal, where her fingerprints had smeared whatever else was there.

3:30 p.m. Tuesday

When she called the hairdresser to see how she was, Suzanne recited the phone number twice from memory before hearing Kayra's voice. For a split second, she didn't recognize it. Several customers chatted in the background about tanning appointments. Suzanne imagined one as flat-chested and friendly, pushing her frosted hair out of her eyes. Another, she was sure, was plump and boasted a bob cut. It was in the lilt of their voices. Kayra's voice, on the other hand, was sonorous, but it was saying something else: "No, they don't know who did it. They couldn't find any fingerprints. It's dear of you, though, to call." And then she rescheduled Suzanne's appointment.

2:28 a.m. Wednesday

Suzanne dreamed of ski-masked men rummaging through drawers of bobby pins and curlers. With their gloved hands, they threw hair clips on the waxed floor, wielded curling irons like swords to knock over bottles of lotion. They hurled aerosol cans of hairspray and cracked every mirror. They smashed open a gumball machine and greedily grabbed quarters. They ripped photos of Kayra's children from their frames on the wall, then stomped on the glossy 5 x 7s with large, muddy boots. Prying open the new cash register with a nail file, they fled with hundreds of bills in their black backpacks.

8:30 a.m. Thursday

Contrary to what the police had first thought, the burglar had not jimmied the front door with a credit card. He had not even come that way. Kayra told her all this as she spun Suzanne around in her chair, checking to make sure she had cut the back straight and snipping away at loose ends. He had come in, the hairdresser explained, through the back door, had first hit an antique store three towns over. The cops got a match on the footprints. And besides that, the thief had dropped directions right there (Kayra pointed toward the mauve chair) to a new cash register he had stolen from the other place. Imagine that? Yes, Suzanne could imagine.

8: 58 a.m. Thursday

She gave Kayra a larger-than-usual tip. At least it was a neat thief, she thought. The place hadn't been trashed, and only a hundred bucks or so were taken. There was, though, the SweetTarts machine, lugged all the way down to the back cellar door and smashed with a hammer, the small circles of color cracked and scattered on the basement floor. She told Kayra about

129

the time her own purse had been stolen. She'd found it later in an alley, the faux-leather discarded, photos ripped from her wallet and tossed in the mud, a large footprint in the middle of her favorite wedding snapshot. That had been years ago when she lived in another state. Still, Kayra said she understood, and kept trimming. When she was just about finished, the hairdresser yanked out—like a mother yanking off her child's Band-Aid— one unruly gray strand from Suzanne's otherwise perfectly coiffed head.

9:03 a.m. Thursday

From the cash register, it was only a few more steps to the front door. Suzanne put her credit card neatly back in her wallet and hugged Kayra goodbye. "They'll find whoever did this," Suzanne said. "They already have the prints." Then, with her hair newly washed, cut, and styled, she headed toward her family van, across the street in the metered parking lot, right where it was supposed to be. The front door swung shut behind her. She wondered if the locks had been replaced, what she would find the next time she entered, and who would be sitting in her chair.

"Some Women Fall in Love With Criminals"

Williamsport Sun-Gazette headline
August 12, 2005

Jilting her husband, the prison psychologist fell in love with an inmate. "You would, too," she explained later, "if you took the time to study his eyes." In them was the trust of his victims.

If you analyze the iris, some spiritualists contend, you'll find flecks of joy and sorrow. Watch where the light goes, how quickly or slowly the pupil dissolves. Have you gone into your lover's brain. What did you find there?

After Ted Bundy's conviction, a flood of women flocked to the courtroom, continued their loyal love letters. During his second trial, Carole Ann said, "I do."

The lifeline on a person's palm, once stained with blood, is hard to clean. However, in such circumstances, persistence works well. How long is your attention span?

Jennifer, a former nurse, ambushed two prison guards as they led her husband, a convicted robber, from his Kentucky hearing. While driving them 185 miles to an Ohio Amway convention, their cab driver heard what they didn't say. "Amway people are all about Amway, and when they didn't try any conversation further about it, that's when I pretty much thought, 'Well, they're not with Amway; they're doing something else.'" He also noted that they didn't tip well.

To get help editing your bestselling novel on bank robbers, first marry a Canadian poet. Next, obtain parole. Third, have two children. Fourth, wait a dozen years. Fifth—and this is important—don't bungle your next burglary.

While holding a gun, check to make sure you have all your fingers and that your wedding band fits correctly. This is also a good time to examine your fingernails and the health of your cuticles. A trip to the drugstore may be necessary and should be accomplished within forty-eight hours.

Three weeks before her twenty-fourth wedding anniversary, the female prison guard got a tattoo that matched her lover's, then helped him escape. "The attempted murder conviction," Vicki explained later, "was simply a misunderstanding."

"The brain can trick itself into believing what the eyes see." Now attach the appropriate cliché about love and blindness.

"Rona Fields, a Washington D.C. psychologist who has worked with prison inmates and staff, said interpersonal relationships in a prison setting can evolve in ways that might seem strange in the outside world." Northeastern University criminologist James Allan Fox, agrees, 'In some cases, it's a question of adding spice to life.'"

According to K. Arvidson of Friberg University, "The number of basic taste qualities registered by single human fungiform papillae is correlated with the number of taste buds borne on the papillae. Multiple sensitivity was demonstrated both in single fungiform papillae and in single taste buds, with response to all four of the basic taste qualities occurring in a single bud."

When cooking, don't be afraid to experiment with unusual spices. The culinary arts are, indeed, an art, and creativity is a necessary ingredient. Read the recipe, but don't be bound by it. Always, always, season to taste.

UPS Guy

3624 Melody Lane

He arrives on Mondays and Thursdays in his pressed, coffee-colored uniform. I have ordered him just so by filling out forms for how-to books, glow-in-the-dark lampshades, automatic toasters, and, of course, fresh coffee. "Order Brown," I hum while pouring my first cup.

I met him by accident after mistakenly choosing a too-large teddy from See-Through Visions. He came with a smirk and a nod, with shoulders broad enough to carry a returned writing desk. His dark hair covered his eyebrows but not his ears. After I charged some Jowell hairdresser scissors, he trimmed it.

Up by dawn, I listen for his large rectangle of a truck. He leaves his door open, so he can see me in my bedroom window. I smile but do not wave. I take my time descending the stairs. I am the highlight of his day. I let him ring the bell three times before I answer. If he wore a hat, he would tip it coming and going.

Sometimes, he doesn't arrive until noon, but I forgive him. To solve the problem, I have ordered him three new watches. One is a Rolex knock-off with a tortoise strap to match his tux. Another is from Walt Disney World: Mickey chasing Minnie around a cherub. He can wear this to our private picnics at Worlds End State Park. The last timepiece is especially designed for our deep-sea diving trips to the Bahamas. He knows they are for him and thanks me twice when I sign his slips. Timing is important. I wait.

3626 Melody Lane.

Every time Postcard, my Chihuahua, hears that gas-hogging truck next door, of course he's going to yap. Wouldn't you? The thing is a monster and all rattle. The only thing I can do is take him out. Let him stretch his little legs. It's hard being so small. It calms him to pee on the tires or go in the neighbor's garden near her marigolds. Good fertilizer, too. But does she thank me? Once she ordered me an aluminum Pooper Scooper with his name on it—Postcard. I sent it back for the refund and got binoculars instead. I'll let you know what I see. As far as I can tell, he never goes in. With her toothpick legs, who'd want to?

3625 Melody Lane.

Though she works odd hours and lives in a small cape cod, that new pretty gal across the street is loaded. I know. At least twice a week, the UPS truck stops near her front walk. I've seen packages as large as refrigerators and as small as ring boxes. Her light is always on, waiting. She takes a long time signing the release. Almost fifty, she wears mail-order negligees, gives women a bad name. Not like my Janie, rest her soul. They're not all spendthrifts, you know. Some of them wait for the mailman for that Social Security check. Now there's a man you can depend on. I should know, having been one for forty years. That was then.

In my day, you'd get your kisses delivered with a stamp. You had to have patience for love and a good writing hand. The boy would win the girl with words. That's where the romance was. How could you wrap the world up with a bow? What sweet nothings could a fellow pen to his girl? What would she write in reply? I smelled perfume on many of the letters I delivered, but was one ever opened? Not a one. We respected privacy back then. You can't buy that by typing on fancy computers. Maybe that's where she works—that eBay place. Must get a discount.

UPS Guy

The job? Well, I could take it or leave it. It's just temporary until my book gets picked up by some big publishing house and all these lonely old gals and know-nothing yuppies will see my name in the stacks at Barnes and Nobles. Funny thing is, right now I'm the one collecting their autographs, if you know what I mean. I put that in the book. The job has its perks like that. You get to thinking things. Like why did a parent choose the name *Syracuse*? Or, does your wife know that you're ordering six fake diamond bracelets? Or, how many times can you ring a doorbell before it wears out?

You can tell which neighbors hate which neighbors on account of how they react when you ask them to take a package. Some are delighted, and you think they might keep the new paisley curtains for themselves. Others whine and complain that it's a one-way relationship since they never get to go away themselves and are always looking after the neighbor's house. They probably pick up the newspapers, too. I tell them to just say no. It's surprising what they tell you about each other. For instance, I found out this way that a priest on Murray Ave. got cut out of his father's will, and that a schoolteacher on Pensacola embezzled from the athletic fund at her school. Go figure.

You also can tell a hell of a lot by the way someone signs a name. Some go all corny on you with hearts and swirls. Some try to make you think they are doctors with their impossible-to-decipher scribbles. Wives sign husbands' names; husbands sign wives' names. I even have a few who sign Marilyn Monroe or Jimmy Stewart—as if I wouldn't notice, although really, it's all the same to me, as long as I can leave the package and go my way.

And there are other perks, too. There's a guy down on Jefferson who saves all his *Playboys* for me, and a few over-the-hillers who put on a little extra lipstick when I come around. I give them a show, sure; what does it hurt? Some broads are lonely and could use a wink now and then. There's this one, a divorcee, I think, who must have stock in Victoria Secret. A nice face, but too bad I can't put some of those Playboy chicks under all that face and lace. It's a shame to waste the fancy stuff on sag and bones. She tries, though, I got to give her that. All gussied up for someone. She doesn't say much, but she orders more than all her neighbors put together. Strange stuff, too. Who really wears a Disney watch where Mickey has a hard-on for Minnie? She showed me that one the next week. Hell if I know what to say. I'm just a guy in brown. All I do is nod and keep delivering.

3624 Melody Lane

For a little extra, you can get Special Saturday Delivery. The first time, I'm not sure if it will be him (he could do the gym weekends, say, or have a second job giving massages. One look at those hands, and I'd sign on). Plus, it's raining and the ledge only covers so much, so he has on one of those brown UPS ponchos with a hood that half covers his face. Once I open the door, though, I know. The way he reaches out his arm. Those hands. Though he's half my age, each of his fingers is twice as long as mine. The fingers of a pianist or a typist. (I confess I've written poems about them.) How can I not imagine them entwined with mine?

Lightning flashes, and—just like that—he pulls back his hood and smiles, the rain pouring down behind him all romantic like in the movies, "best service and lowest rates" scrolling across my mind. I'm just about to ask him in when he turns and waves to that widow next door, Mrs. McSomething, the one who won't control her Chihuahua. She's out walking the little yapper, even in this downpour, and wouldn't you know it, she's got a matching tiny raincoat on his skinny body. She holds an umbrella over him as he pees on my pansies.

3626 Melody Lane

Even under the umbrella, the binoculars fog up in the rain. I wipe the lenses with a tissue while keeping Postcard covered. He catches cold easily, but I need him. Together, we can sniff out the good stories, get close to the real doings. That one next door who claims to have been a model but got fired for getting old, that one, OK, I admit it, sometimes I feel sorry even for her. Not a dog to keep her company. Buys and buys and buys because her heart is empty. I know. She's still trying to wiggle her hips for the delivery boy. I don't know his name, but I call him Hank in my *roman* à *clef,* the one they'll publish when I die, a real page-turner that will shock the neighbors. I had to make up what I couldn't see, of course, poetic license and all, but I know exactly how it will end and who the readers will be. I've left detailed instructions in my will. I want a cover with one of those grocery-store heroines slaving over a typewriter with a dog asleep on the floor of a candlelit room. I want my name in red on the spine. *Rainy Day Romance* I'm calling it. The proceeds will go to Postcard.

3625 Melody Lane

One day I get so tired of that truck rattling out front and that all-alone curvy gal across the street coming out in little more than her underwear that I decide to write her a letter. I took a calligraphy class at the Forkville Community Retirement Center last March and need some practice anyway. After I get the pen, ink, and instructions sheet out, though, I look a while at Janie's photo, the one where we are camping in the rain over by Logan. She's drenched but smiling. When we weren't loving, we wrote postcards while the rain pattered on top of the guaranteed waterproof tent. What a script she had—beautiful, long letters and easy to read. She could fit more on a postcard and have it mean something than anyone I know. And her love letters to me—these kids today don't know the meaning of romance. You got to create anticipation. Let me tell you, those are the days that come back to you in your old age.

I stare again at the black-and-white print, then say, "Maybe I'm being too hard on her, Janie. I know what lonely's like. Can't say I don't. Eats at you. Maybe I'm just an old-fashioned softie like you always said. Maybe I am." I re-arrange the pen, paper, and instructions sheet three times on my writing desk. Finally, I sit down and begin. *Dear Miss,* (obviously, she isn't married) *I am enclosing a copy of Elizabeth Barrett Browning's tender love poems.* I spill a bit of ink under one of the g's but turn the smudge into a small heart, making it all swirly.

Looking over what I've done so far, I add at the end of *tender love poems* the words to her husband with a fancy underline and some curlicues. Maybe that will soften her up a bit, let her know that some of us are the settling-down types. I pull my used copy that Janie gave me from its spot on the fireplace mantel. Its cover is worn, and some of the pages are dog-eared. I run my fingers over the gold trim on the cover. I memorized all the words twenty years back. Still, I take a moment just to hold it. I like how it feels in my hands. Like love. "I'm banking on getting it back," I say to myself or the photo; I'm not sure which.

Carefully, I wrap it in leftover United Postal Service tissue paper that I've been saving. Didn't know why until now. I tuck the ends over, nice like. Then I go back to my writing desk and add to the letter. *These poems were given to me by someone I loved very much. Shall we read them together?*

I'm surprised at myself, but continue anyways. Who says women are the only ones who can change their minds? I decide to go whole hog then and sketch two cherubs chasing each other across the bottom edge.

How to sign? That's always the question. I stumble over that a bit, then simply put *Henry.* Straightforward. I know I'm twenty years her senior, but I'm as dependable as the mail (literally), and you couldn't get much closer. Just thirty steps to cross the street. No way of getting lost. I put both the tissue-wrapped book and the note in a brown box (another leftover from my route days), then slip that into a plastic grocery bag. Everyone knows you can't trust that UPS. I'll deliver it by hand later when she's not watching. A little bit of mystery makes the romance, I always say.

UPS Guy

The rain's coming down like cats and dogs now (how do those old fogey mailmen deal with this shit year after year?), and I oversleep and am only now starting my Saturday deliveries. Already an hour behind. The extra cash is good, yeah, but I'm drenched from the first few stops. They can't wait two days and save the dough? Every woman who's just bought something wants to chat and tell you all about it. My mouth is sore from smiling. I'm up for the role play most days, but who in his right mind can be in a good mood in this weather? Can't they hear that thunder? What do they think? I have time to stand in the rain and giggle? Twenty houses to go. I swear, once the snow hits, I'm outta this gig. No life-long postal vow for me. That truck is a drunk skunk on skates.

3624 Melody Lane

An hour after Mrs—what's her name again?— distracts my guy and postpones everything, I hear her Chihuahua making another ruckus. At first, I think he's right outside my door, but by the time I get off the computer and to the front of the house, both the dog and that snoopy neighbor are up on the sidewalk. It's just drizzling, but the dog still dons that silly raincoat. He probably keeps the old gal happy, though, I say to myself, and am surprised to find myself smiling. I shiver a bit and pull on a terry cloth robe from the hall closet.

I clear off a circle of fog from the front door window and watch them, a perfect pair, really, as they step together under her large, black umbrella. Both skinny and nervous. The books are right; owners and their pets do resemble each other. Maybe there's something to having a dog curled up there on the floor keeping you company while you're typing away on your computer. Maybe.

I start to turn back to my coffee and my own half-written novel when I catch a glimpse of something on the front step just under the small over-hang. It's a plastic grocery bag, and for a moment I think I've forgotten that I'd ordered a delivery.

When I take it inside, though, I discover a plain brown mailing box. Inside, wrapped neatly in postal tissue paper, is a book by my favorite poet. I can hear myself taking three deep breaths. Then again. I pull my robe tighter and back away from the door. How could I not have heard him? Sometime in the last hour, he'd come back.

3626 Melody Lane
Postcard is taking her time: first eating her brunch of Purina Dog Chow and my leftover toast, then nursing a mailbox chew toy. I get a good hour in on *Rainy Day Romance* before she nips at my ankles, then tries to put her paws up in my lap. It's a wonder I ever get a page done. Turns out, though, she's done me a favor. With our umbrella and matching raincoats,

I take her back, the way she likes, to the neighbor's flowerbed. But this time she's not interested. It's then I notice the plastic bag hung on the neighbor's doorknob, half-on, half-off like it's going to splat in the small puddle below. Naturally, that won't do. Postcard and I pitter-patter our way over there. I'm about to ring the bell when I happen to notice the brown mailer inside. Book-sized. A note card has fallen out of the box and is loose in the plastic. Just as Postcard and I guessed. Of course, I tuck it back in. While I'm doing that favor, I can't help but notice the name Henry in fancy script. Soon, I think to myself, he'll shorten it to Hank.

And because he is young and should know better but doesn't, I put the bag safely under the small front overhang. "Don't they teach them anything at that UPS?" I whisper to Postcard.

3625 Melody Lane

Of course, I expect a reply by mail. Did I mention that I included a stamp? That will take at least a day, but, really, it's worth the wait. All that mystery just to end up right across the street. It's exciting, sure.

After my second cup of coffee and three chapters of Dickens, I check again and, yes, the bag is gone and a back light on, at least I think that's where the glow comes from. Of course, it will take a while for her to compose a reply, but not long to guess the sender. I introduced myself when she first moved in, tried to help her with that computer of hers though the writing desk was too heavy for this old heart. (That doesn't mean it's not alive and well in the ways that count. Right, Janie?)

O dear God, I hope she's not typing her answer.

Learning to Yell

Backwards Chronology

SHE WAS YELLING FROM the top of a cliff. Her voice echoed back to her as strange. She was yelling from her daughter's bedroom. Everywhere she stepped was a half-clothed Barbie doll or a marble. Underneath a pile of discarded clothes, a CD player rapped. Her voice echoed back to her as strange.

Earlier (think years, think another life) she'd stood in that L-shaped bedroom on 5th and Park, the shadow of his arm raised, her vocal chords as yet untrained. (Practice the letters of your own name, then raise the volume.)

She listened back further to parents unwilling to shout, their disagreements always between lines, subtle, silent, her own young face looking up into the argument, confused and unable to help. There was no swearing, no hitting. When she misspoke (never with voice raised), she was reprimanded immediately, even before the end of the sentence. When she opened her mouth, no understanding came out, not even a squeak of sentience.

Then

In such silence, she wrote a life, tried on the words that fit, and erased the others. She married a man who read. When he yelled, he used entire sentences and waited for her to answer.

Together, they learned to climb mountains. Rock. Dirt. Fear. Breath. Rock. Sometimes, up high, all she heard was the past. Most often, not. It was too much effort remembering what was. Miles up, who could tell the difference between laughter and lies? It was better to breathe in the new.

After a decade, she began to recognize her own voice, even when whispering from the edge of a cliff.

Before Then

"This is how you do it," she read in the kit she ordered over eBay. "Open your lungs and lips. Let the past pour out." But in the midst of those bruises on 5th and Park, she had been too scared to practice. Something got caught behind her teeth. She thinks it was her soul.

She tried to remember how others did it, but all she could picture were TV dramas with the volume turned low. The make-believe characters were always flailing their arms, trying to untangle anger. Underneath the red of their faces, she wondered if they were having fun, if pride were rising up in their throats.

When she tried to tell this to her mother, one day in June long distance over the phone, another story came out. It was a voice on the other end she didn't recognize that claimed her mother's name. Guilt was how it described the one time she had yelled, her words flung hot and fierce out the kitchen window at a neighbor girl bullying her daughter. "I was so ashamed of myself," her mother's distant voice exclaimed, then died down into a whisper.

"Ashamed to help me?" the now-grown daughter managed to ask before the phone clicked dead. It seemed too late to re-dial.

Now

"Listen to me," her nine-year-old daughter yelled, "For once, would you just listen to me?" She recognized her daughter's voice as her own, but younger and stronger.

It rose up, a crescendo of pride, unafraid to fall. Atop that mountain of words was her girl. The past was far below, a mere murmur.

What could she do but applaud, listen for the echo of joy?

Squirrelly in PA

cunningly unforthcoming or reticent (thefreedictionary.com)

unpredictable or jumpy. . . eccentric (allwords.com)

an offensive term meaning very irrational or odd. . .characteristic of squirrels
(encarta.msn.com/dictionary)

I.

THE FLYERS STUN US, spreading their limbs until skin becomes a sail. After a leap and a glide, they parachute among green. Tightrope walkers extraordinaire, they balance on telephone wires, then dive to swinging twigs barely strong enough to hold berries.

Touting their tails like parasols, the gray are the playful pranksters of our youth, the daredevils we no longer dream ourselves becoming. Arrogant bandits, they tiptoe across backyard fences; clenched between their teeth lie bagels, tea bags, and hot dog buns from nearby garbage pails. They scale bird feeders and steal old corncobs, invade attics, and dig up bulbs. These paradoxical pals amuse and irritate us. We want to be like them. We hate what they are.

II.

Then there are the extraordinary, those bright in their whiteness who prance across small-town college campuses and nibble peanuts from our extended palms. Entranced, we praise the albino, delight in the red of its eyes. Its rarity is a prize we crave. For hours, we sit on benches, watching them watch us. We click our tongues and call to them. We organize clubs to spot them. We donate funds to charity in their name.

III.

An overgrown Eagle Scout, my father once hunted squirrel—not in the woods, but on the rectangle lawn of our suburban backyard. That day, I did not hear the crack of my father's shotgun. I still envision the squirrels as unsuspecting, barking no warnings to each other, teasing him with their scampers. Our yard was, after all, their claimed territory. They knew the trees much better than we. When I'd rest in the limbs of our maple to read, they'd eye me like a distant relative. When my mother pulled weeds, they'd race between shrubs playing hide-and-seek. When my father cut the lawn, they'd scurry through the clippings like slapstick comedians. They made it clear that it was their good humor that allowed us to remain.

It was only later at the dinner table—after the first bite of meat—that my father told the story of the meal, only then that I learned to swallow betrayal.

IV.

Always a mother, I break for does crossing our oak-lined streets. My minivan, crammed with children, has learned to slow for chipmunks and raccoons. Most often, though, it's the squirrels, brazen in their jaywalking, that control traffic. Here I meet the neighbors, all in our cars, waiting for the bushy-tailed to signal the go ahead, to tell us all is safe. Only then do we cross to the rest of our lives.

V.

At nine, my athlete son fears bikes, the skinned knees and over-the-handle-bar flips he swears they threaten. He's left his bravado at the ball field. Still, one cool day, I tempt him with after-the-ride treats of ice cream. I lure him to our local rails-to-trails where wide asphalt and barely existent inclines make room for his wobbly attempts.

At first, his body is at a forty-five-degree angle, balancing the obstinate frame of red steel. Later, upright, he's quarreling with a rebellious chain that slips whenever he captures confidence. Finally, by mid-morning, he's barreling over the transformed tracks, his legs churning a type of flight, his sunburnt face grinning fun. This is the happiness I've been waiting for, the joy that whips back his hair and lets him breathe his grown-up freedom.

It's a squirrel that does us in. My son, pedaling pell-mell, tilts his front wheel toward the bike path's only tunnel. It's then the creature darts, zig-zags, darts again, then stops shock-still in the bike's path. What can nine years teach a boy but to swerve and avoid fur? He forgets the tunnel wall won't budge, won't applaud his speed.

When handlebars and teeth hit concrete, my son's wail is wild. The unre-pentant rodent swishes its tail and stares. "Stupid squirrel," my son screams, a small boy again, as he hobbles back, fear returned, toward suburbia.

Pennsylvania Round in Four Parts

I.

BEFORE PENNSYLVANIA, THE WORLD was flat, the distance between two horizons a straight view. In those other states, I walked a state-of-mind, linear but un-livable. Map coordinates located something less than inhale/exhale. Now place has something to do with oxygen horded in the limbs of hemlock and elm, with the way these mountains bulge with breath. Air blooms among such unbashful blues and greens, darts with the dragonfly, and drinks with the white-tailed deer. Always, it winds with the creeks, then glides over Allegheny curves to rise up with the hawks. When the firefly blinks, it is not an SOS but a refrain from a mountain song so old you can hear the hills humming.

II.

The only light in the shotgun house is the steady blink of the TV. I've swept her job at the mill beneath the corners of a forty-year-old carpet, crammed his factory work in the closet they no longer open. But for years, I couldn't ignore the hum of what they didn't have, the absence they gave my husband in abundance. I can almost touch each wall with its peeling paper of orange watering cans as I hike between sheet-covered furniture lined up for the one clear view of a sitcom. Though I try to get comfortable, I can't. Even the air bunches up against itself between straight planes of plaster.

Outside the narrow windows, bricks block the coal-tinged breeze. Rusting lawn chairs clutter the neighbors' crumbling porches from which out-of-work, middle-aged men stare at each other and do nothing. Teens compete at squealing their makeshift hot rods down the thin strip of asphalt leftover between tightly parked pick-ups and hand-me-down four-doors. From the cracked sidewalk, barefoot girls in midriffs pause their hopscotch and wave.

I head instead to their backyard, where blooms border a six-by-four yard and spill over as geraniums and pansies, roses and black-eyed Susans, tulips and marigolds. Humming birds nip nectar. Tomatoes bob from stalks tied-up with old panty hose. Lettuce proclaims victory over rabbits, and strawberries congratulate themselves for against-the-odds growth. My brown thumb, envious to the end, fingers joy.

III.

The doe and its fawn enter our backyard on the slant, kitty-corner themselves from rhododendron bush to magnolia. Theirs is a quiet joy, stepping just so from their hills into suburbia, the distance six hops of a skipped stone. They've forgotten to worry and remember this grass and the long limbs of our maple. They step easily between swing set and tool shed, detour around a half-finished game of croquet. Nurtured on grace, they politely turn their sleek necks to avoid our gaze. From behind glass, my children stare. They compare the soft sheen of the deer's fur to sketched likenesses in store-bought books. My husband warns them not to open the door, not to let the conditioned air out.

IV.

Beneath the tent flaps, my children and I breathe in the wild Pennsylvania air. The mountains, we say, are hugging the wind, the laurel so thick we could pick a thousand blooms. All evening we count the blinks of fireflies. We sense hawks circling the night clouds above our camp and bears obediently pausing between the zigzags of evergreens. We listen long into the dark until the drone of crickets leads us into dreams full of deer and ruffed grouse. Then we doze without worry, the curve of the world huddled about us as we breathe its crispness in.

In the chilled morning air, when we emerge from sleep and the tent door, it is—almost-surprisingly—just our backyard on the outside, our hammock waiting in the half-light of dawn. We think we hear the doe and her fawn, but it is my husband up on the patio, already flipping blueberry pancakes on the griddle. The country-style bacon sizzles with joy when we join him, humming our campfire rounds.

And Then

THE NIGHT SHE TURNED forty, she stopped speaking.

Not the morning filled with midlife babies tugging jean hems and black-and-tan puppies gnawing faded pink slippers. Not midday with CNN jab-jab-jabbering in the background as she dusted pollen from newly painted porch furniture. Not the afternoon with her husband outside sautéing tilapia, the acquaintances raising high their Sam Adams to toast her. Not then.

Not even in early evening, congratulations settling into a buzz the height of the hedge, insects still flicks in the less-than-bright light from a fading spring sun. The lure of flesh and feasting not yet on the horizon, the knowledge there.

(As you read this, turn around three times and clap your hands. Were you there? Were you laughing, your voice tangling in the apple buds? May is cheery for the blind and non-asthmatic, an open door of aroma, age swollen into a bloom, years swishing high in the twigs. Hard to breathe anything but sound, the air stuffed with snaps and rustles, ticks and trills. On top of this, human voices, that continuous crescendo.)

Then the guests gone, their over-the-hill jokes packed up in SUVs, puppies yapping at tire spins, other lean bodies clattering away on bikes. The closest neighbors clicking the back gate shut, waving, discussing not-quietly enough—how it went, how she looked.

After that, naturally, the moon was swinging up over the fence, its squinty smile ambiguous. The world continued. Of course, there were the tucking-into-bed hugs with arms smaller than she remembered. There was the lovemaking, sweet and salty.

Not then, either. Does it matter the moment? After the day. Suddenly. Unplanned. Waiting. And then she began to write.

Notes

"Crowned" was a finalist for The Lascaux Prize in Short Fiction 2015.

"Seagulls" was nominated for a 1995 Pushcart Prize by *The American Literary Review*.

In 2003 and 2004, soldiers Jessica Lynch and Lynndie England, both from West Virginia, landed in the media's spotlight. Through the fictional lens of "Soldier Girl," I examine the role that media and gender play in both tragedies, as well as how society rationalizes violence and excuses voyeurism that encircle both victims and perpetrators. The short story draws on interview excerpts and information found in Paul D. Colford and Corky Siemasko's "Fiends Raped Jessica, Book Reveals Shocker/Ex-POW Can't Recall the Assault/I'm Not a Hero, She Says," in a 6 November 2003 article in the *New York Daily News*; the 12 May 2004 CBS News stories "Female GI in Abuse Photos Talks" and "The Pictures: Lynndie England" (Dan Rather on Pfc. Lynndie England); and John Kampfner's "The Truth about Jessica" in the 15 May 2003 of *The Guardian*. Quotations by Jessica Lynch and Lynndie England are woven throughout "Soldier Girl," and for this I gratefully acknowledge CBS News, *The Guardian*, and the *New York Daily News*.

"A Wave Rushed Over" won the 2007 *US Catholic* Fiction Prize.

"*A Doll's House* Redux" is based on Henrik Ibsen's play *A Doll's House*, which premiered in 1879 at the Royal Theatre in Copenhagen, Denmark.

"The Wives" is written from the points of view of the wives of famous characters/men named Peter. In an earlier form, "The Wives" appeared as part of the collection *Wives' Tales* (Seven Kitchens Press); the excerpts "Peter, Peter," "Piper," and "Rabbit" won the 1993 *Seattle Review's* Bentley Prize for Poetry.)

Brief excerpts of Sylvia Plath's poem "The Applicant" are woven throughout the story "Best Face Forward."

"For Real" won the 2007 Sport Literature Association Fiction Award.

"Rachel Isum Robinson: Snatches and Excerpts" was inspired in part by Rachel Robinson's book *Jackie Robinson: An Intimate Portrait*. I also drew on family stories. As the great grandniece of Branch Rickey—the general manager of the Brooklyn Dodgers who helped break the color barrier by signing Jackie Robinson—I grew up with tales of my great granduncle, the Robinsons, and their "Great Experiment," a courageous and necessary venture that shaped not only their lives, but history as well. A brief excerpt of "Blues in the Night," famously recorded by Ella Fitzgerald, appears in the section "Rachel Mourns."

"Watching *42* at the Dollar Matinee with My Mother" references the 2013 movie *42*, written and directed by Brian Helgeland and starring Chadwick Boseman as Jackie Robinson, Nicole Beharie as Rachel Robinson, and Harrison Ford as Branch Rickey.

"Woman's First Skydive Turns Out to be Her Last" is based on a 15 August 2005 *Williamsport Sun-Gazette* article in which eyewitnesses give their account of this tragedy.

"Nonsmoking Section" was nominated for a 2011 Pushcart Prize by *The Minnesota Review.*

"Eiffel Tower" uses excerpts from various Paris travel brochures. It was a finalist for the Gertrude Stein Award in Fiction 2015, sponsored by *The Doctor T. J. Eckleburg Review.*

"Some Women Fall in Love with Criminals" is based on the 12 August 2005 *Williamsport Sun-Gazette* article "Manipulation, Self-deception Involved When Women Fall for Hard-core Criminals" with additional quotations from the 12 August 2005 *New York Times* article "Cabbie Recounts Fugitives' 115-Mile Ride" and the 15 August 1980 *Science* article by K. Arvidson entitled "Human Taste: Response and Taste Bud Number in Fungiform Papillae."

Fomite

A fomite is a medium capable of transmitting infectious organisms from one individual to another.

"The activity of art is based on the capacity of people to be infected by the feelings of others." Tolstoy, What Is Art?

Writing a review on Amazon, Good Reads, Shelfari, Library Thing or other social media sites for readers will help the progress of independent publishing. To submit a review, go to the book page on any of the sites and follow the links for reviews. Books from independent presses rely on reader to reader communications.

For more information or to order any of our books, visit http://www.fomitepress.com/FOMITE/Our_Books.html

Nothing Beside Remains
Jaysinh Birjépatil

The Way None
of This Happened
Mike Breiner

Summer on the
Cold War Planet
Paula Closson Buck

Foreign Tales of
Exemplum and Woe
J. C. Ellefson

Free Fall/Caída libre
Tina Escaja

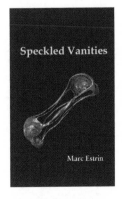

Speckled Vanities
Marc Estrin

Fomite

Off to the Next Wherever
John Michael Flynn

Derail This Train Wreck
Daniel Forbes

Semitones
Derek Furr

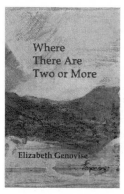

Where There Are Two or More
Elizabeth Genovise

*Snake in the Spine,
Wolf in the Heart*
Barry Goldensohn

*The Three Lives
of Jonathan Force*
Richard Hawley

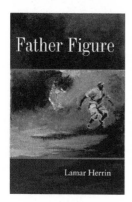

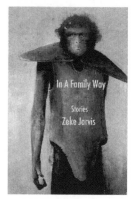

Father Figure
Lamar Herrin

The Fall of Athens
Gail Holst-Warhaft

In A Family Way
Zeke Jarvis

Fomite

A Rising Tide of People
Swept Away
Scott Archer Jones

A Free, Unsullied Land
Maggie Kast

Shadowboxing With
Bukowski
Darrell Kastin

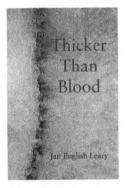

Feminist on Fire
Coleen Kearon

Thicker Than Blood
Jan English Leary

A Guide
to the Western Slopes
Roger Lebovitz

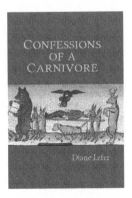

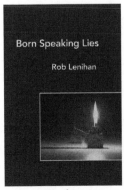

Confessions of a Carnivore
Diane Lefer

Born Speaking Lies
Rob Lenihan

Unborn Children of
America
Michele Markarian

Fomite

Interrogations
Martin Ott

Connecting the Dots
to Shangrila
Joseph D. Reich

Shirtwaist
Delia Bell Robinson

Isles of the Blind
Robert Rosenberg

What We Do For Love
Ron Savage

Bread & Sentences
Peter Schumann

Faust 3
Peter Schumann

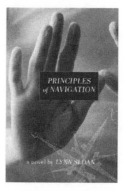

Principles of Navigation
Lynn Sloan

A Great Fullness
Bob Sommer

Fomite

To Join the Lost
Seth Steinzor

Among the Lost
Seth Steinzor

Industrial Oz
Scott T. Starbuck

Among Angelic Orders
Susan Thomas

A Day in the Life
Tom Walker

*The Inconveniece
of the Wings*
Silas Dent Zobal

Fomite

More Titles from Fomite...

Fomite

Made in the USA
Columbia, SC
14 May 2017